SLAVE TO THE NIGHT

THE BROTHERHOOD SERIES - BOOK 2

ADELE CLEE

This is a work of fiction. All names, characters, places and incidents are products of the author's imagination. All characters are fictitious and any resemblance to real persons, living or dead, is purely coincidental.

ISBN-13: 978-0-9932832-9-1

Cover designed by **Jay Aheer**

Dad,
Who taught me from an early age the value and importance of books.
This one's for you.
With love.

CHAPTER 1

With trembling fingers, Grace Denton handed the invitation to the sour-faced majordomo and tried to offer a confident smile. He raised his bushy brows before studying the neat script. Thank the Lord she had the luxury of wearing a mask. It afforded anonymity while certain parts of her anatomy were blatantly exposed for all to see. Never in her life had she imagined baring so much flesh. Her breasts were almost bursting out of her sister's scandalous gown.

Under the servant's hawk-like gaze, she felt her control waver as doubt pushed to the fore.

What was she thinking?

No one would believe she was Caroline. It took more than a striking similarity to assume someone's identity. Her sister oozed confidence in every situation. Whereas Grace blushed like a berry whenever she felt nervous. Caroline spoke with poise and eloquence. Whereas she often rambled and muttered to herself and was prone to saying the wrong thing entirely.

"Enjoy your evening, miss."

"I'm sure I will," she replied, despite fearing it was highly inappropriate to converse with the servants.

As she stepped into the ballroom, she gasped in awe at the

vibrant spectacle. The crowd shone in their flamboyant costumes, and she struggled to absorb the dazzling array of colours. Etiquette be damned at a masquerade, she thought, as milkmaids danced with knights and bishops, and an Oriental princess partnered a sea captain.

Pushing through the crowd, she breathed a sigh of relief. She'd climbed the first obstacle, and now her toes were wedged into the foothold, even if she was dangling precariously from a precipice and could easily flounder.

Once the wife of a gentleman, she knew how to conduct herself in formal situations. But her education had taken place at garden parties and provincial assemblies. She had no real experience when it came to mingling with the aristocracy.

Her older sister, Caroline, had been in London for a year—as a paid companion to an elderly matron, or so Grace had thought. Even Mrs. Whitman had been fooled. Else, despite Grace being a widow of three-and-twenty, she would never have left her in Caroline's care.

Grace caught her reflection in one of the long mirrors lining the wall. The candlelight rebounded off the glass and cast a golden glow over her surprisingly voluptuous figure, squashed into the medieval-inspired gown. From the neck down she appeared exactly like all the other ladies: elegant and sophisticated with an air of wicked sensuality.

From the neck up, things hadn't quite gone to plan.

She had singed a few tendrils with the curling iron. They were crispy, and the smoky aroma invaded her nostrils whenever she turned her head. What had started out as an elaborate coiffure looked more like a poorly made bird nest. The pearl hair comb had slipped down and was digging into the back of her ear.

Hesitant feet caused her to amble around the ballroom. More than a few people turned their heads to acknowledge her. The mole on her left cheek—in the same place as Caroline's—coupled with her fiery red hair no doubt convinced them of her identity. Yet despite feigning an air of composure, inside she felt like a child in a room full of hungry wolves.

Grace knew the name of her quarry, but nothing more. One word from the dissipated lord would confirm what she needed to know. After spending a lifetime with Caroline, she recognised the language of a liar, although she had no skill when it came to the mannerisms of a murderer.

"Caroline. There you are. I've been looking everywhere for you."

The warm, feminine voice caught her off guard. Grace swung around with a gasp, her fingers fluttering to her throat and coming to rest on the topaz necklace—another of her sister's prized possessions.

"Why, am I late?" Grace knew her voice lacked confidence, knew the lady before her was a stranger.

"No," the lady replied, her curious gaze roaming over Grace's hair. "You're not late. But Barrington is looking for you, and he is not best pleased. I thought I ought to warn you."

Grace recalled no mention of a Barrington in her sister's diary. There had been a whole host of unseemly tales regarding other gentlemen, so she had to suppose this man lacked the skills necessary to capture Caroline's attention.

Guilt flared.

Reading the evidence of someone's innermost thoughts was a gross invasion of privacy. She'd spent a whole day holding the book in her hands before finally deciding to peel back the cover and peer inside.

"And what have I done to warrant Barrington's displeasure?" Now she sounded far too haughty.

Oh, this was never going to work.

A frown marred the lady's brow. "Don't be coy. You know full well you were to meet him at the theatre last night. But looking at the state of your hair, it's clear you're not well."

"I do feel a little out of sorts." Feigning illness would go some way to account for her character flaws. And it gave her a perfect opportunity to broach the subject of her quarry. "I would have stayed at home tonight, but I need to speak to Lord Markham."

The lady made an odd puffing sound. "Markham? Don't waste your time. You know his rule about never bedding the same woman twice." She stepped closer. "Was he so good you would risk facing rejection?"

What was she supposed to say to that?

"He … he was so good I'd ride backwards on a donkey and cry *tallyho* just for another chance."

The lady screwed up her nose and then giggled. "What's wrong with you tonight? You're normally so serious."

"My heart's all jittery thinking about Lord Markham. Where is he? Have you seen him this evening?"

"He's standing near the alcove. Markham's the only gentleman in the room not in costume, so you're unlikely to miss him." The lady placed her hand on Grace's arm. "What are you going to do about Barrington? He will not tolerate your blasé attitude. Without the protection of a gentleman, he can make things difficult for you."

Grace did not have to worry about Barrington and neither did Caroline, not anymore.

"I'll do what I always do," she said, attempting to sound vain. "I shall smile and flutter my lashes and all will be well."

In their youth, Caroline had used the trick a hundred times or more.

"Oh, you're incorrigible. Let me know how you fare with Lord Markham, although I'm sure to hear tales of your humiliation. I may even rouse the courage to try myself."

As Grace walked away, she was overcome by a wave of sadness. Was this how Caroline spent her time? Comparing conquests and juggling suitors? There was something shallow, something degrading about succumbing to the voracious demands of men.

Where had it all gone wrong?

After reading the diary, she had a fair idea.

There was only one gentleman wearing evening clothes. He was conversing with a man dressed in the garb of a Turkish prince, whose crimson pantaloons were attracting much female attention.

Lord Markham, or so she assumed, had the bearing of a man who bowed to no one. Dressed all in black, he exuded raw masculinity. With his arrogant chin, sinful mouth and lethal gaze he embodied all the qualities she imagined of a scandalous rake. His decision to forgo a mask made him appear all the more masterful, all the more dangerous.

Grace swallowed down her nerves and tried to muster just an ounce of her sister's steely composure. It was the height of rudeness to interrupt a conversation and so she hovered at his side in the hope he would notice her.

The first thing he did notice were her breasts and his lustful gaze lingered there for longer than necessary. Grace could feel her cheeks flame under his scrutiny. Her instincts cried for her to flee, the feeling only tempered by her sheer desperation to discover what the gentleman knew.

His expression altered dramatically as his gaze drifted up to the topaz necklace, up to the mole on her cheek. Recognition dawned, and his countenance resumed the same tired, world-weary air.

"Ah, Miss Rosemond," he said, glancing down at her breasts once more. "I see you have found a way to enhance the paltry assets bestowed upon you. Some poor devil will have a fright when his hand curls around a pair of old stockings."

The gentleman's mouth was as foul as his reputation. Trust him to notice the only distinct difference. And why had he called her Rosemond? Had he mistaken her for someone else or had Caroline used a different name? More importantly, he showed not the slightest surprise at her presence.

"You presume to know me, my lord," she said, trying not to show her displeasure at his derogatory remark. He apparently felt within his rights to speak in such base terms, and she felt another pang of sadness for the sweet sister she once knew.

The Turkish prince sniggered, his turban wobbling back and forth, but became distracted when a lady stopped to admire the softness of his silk trousers.

Lord Markham raised an arrogant brow. "I know you a little too well, I fear."

Grace lifted her chin. "How so? I find such a critical assessment causes my memory to fail me." She was doing far better than she ever hoped and resisted the urge to clap her hands. After all, such a dire situation was not to be trivialised.

"When it comes to the weaknesses of the flesh, my memory never fails me."

Grace smiled. "I'm afraid I can only recall the things I deem important."

Lord Markham narrowed his gaze, and his mouth twitched at the corners. "Then tell me what you do remember."

The request caught her by surprise.

How was she supposed to answer that?

"I—I couldn't p-possibly repeat it."

Oh, God, she was going to start mumbling.

Lord Markham turned fully and focused his attention, gazing deeply through the oval holes of her mask into her eyes. The room appeared to sway, and she sucked in a breath to calm the flutter in her heart.

"Oh, I think you can," he said. The amber flecks in his green eyes grew more prominent. His gloved finger came to rest on her pendant, drifted seductively over the topaz stones. Grace shivered at his touch and his mouth curved up into a satisfied smile. "Tell me what you imagine occurred between us. Tell me."

Grace swallowed. "I … I won't repeat it."

He leant forward. The smell of pine and some other earthy masculine fragrance bombarded her senses. "Tell me." He dropped his hand as his greedy gaze dipped to her breasts bulging out from the neckline of her gown. "Whisper the words to me."

Little streams of light blurred her vision, forcing her to blink rapidly. Her mind felt fuzzy, as though a dense fog had settled to obscure all rational thought. All she could think of was how it felt to lie naked with a man.

But not just any man—with Lord Markham.

Good heavens.

Beads of perspiration formed on her brow, and she touched her fingers to her forehead as strange words unwittingly entered her thoughts.

But there was murder afoot. She was convinced of it. The thought gave her the strength to fight whatever weird and wonderful notions filled her head.

She was here for Caroline. Nothing else mattered.

"I—I don't remember anything," she whispered, her breath coming short and quick as she dismissed the image of her eager fingers roaming over his muscular chest.

The muscle in his cheek twitched. He jerked his head back with a look of utter bewilderment. Had no one ever refused his request? Knowing she had the power to knock the arrogance out of him gave her the courage to be bold.

"Nor will I waste my time or imagination pandering to your warped sense of curiosity. If you're looking for someone to indulge your fantasies, I suggest you try …" Her mind went blank. Where do gentlemen find women to frolic with, other than at a ball? "Try the … the market."

It was the first thing that popped into her head. You could buy everything at the market, why not women?

Lord Markham's eyes widened. "The market?"

While her blood rushed through her veins at a rapid rate, it took a detour past her cheeks, choosing her ears to convey her embarrassment. She could feel them swelling, throbbing and burning. If she were to touch them with wet fingers, they would most certainly sizzle.

"I am a viscount," he continued with an indolent wave. "I do not need to trawl the markets looking for someone to warm my bed, as well you know."

"Forgive me," she said, overcome with a desperate need to wipe the smirk off his face. "What else was I supposed to think when you have the mouth of a sewer rat?"

"This is an interesting game," he said, showing no sign of offence. "I cannot recall the last time my mind was as stimulated as my—"

"I do not need to hear more of your vulgarity."

He put his hand on his chest and laughed. "My vulgarity? Have you cared to glance in the mirror? Your hair gives the impression that you've recently been tumbled. Your gown is far too small and at any moment I am in danger of being blinded. Your lips are red and swollen from—"

"It is rouge," she said, thrusting her hands on her hips. At least, she hoped that's what was in the silver cachou box. Their mother had often said such things were nought but selfish vanity to mask a weak mind. "And I have put on weight since I last wore this dress. There is nothing vulgar or lewd about any of it."

"Are you not a courtesan, Caroline? Do you not openly court vulgarity?"

Grace suppressed a gasp upon hearing her sister's name pass from his lips. She knew the depths of Caroline's disgrace but saying it so openly made it seem so crude, so terribly heart-breaking.

"I am a lady, my lord," she said, unable to control the anger that infused her tone, "and I ask you to have a care. I have tolerated your uncouth manner for long enough."

When he smiled, she knew she had made a mistake.

Lord Markham bowed. "Please accept my humble apology." There was not even a hint of sarcasm in his tone. A shiver raced down her spine as she suspected her worst fear was about to come to fruition. "I'm afraid your deception forced me to be blunt."

"M-my deception? Now you're speaking in riddles, my lord."

"Despite wearing her necklace, I think we both know you're not Caroline Rosemond. The question is, who the hell are you and what do you want with me?"

CHAPTER 2

Elliot watched the lady's lips move, but no words came out. He had seen through her guise almost instantly. Even a king's hosier with access to the finest silk stockings couldn't pad a corset sufficiently to make small breasts appear so deliciously soft and plump.

Indeed, he was still trying to determine his mood. Aroused by the lady's witty banter, was he angry he'd not get the chance to bed her? Angered by her deception, was it the need to command and conquer that caused desire to ignite?

Either way, anger and desire whirled around inside to leave him both frustrated and highly irritable.

"Let us find somewhere a little more private." He cupped her elbow, his grip firm as he steered her towards the terrace.

"Where are we going?" she said, tottering along beside him, and he could hear the nervous flutter in her voice. Caroline Rosemond would have offered a flirtatious remark, suggesting she was game for whatever vigorous pursuit he had in mind. But there was always a price, and he'd never been willing to pay.

"To find somewhere quiet so we can talk."

The lady mumbled to herself, her words softer than a whisper.

When he reached the doors leading out to the garden, she shrugged out of his grasp. "We can't go out there. What if someone should see us?"

"You forget that the majority of the guests will assume you're Caroline Rosemond. Trust me. She would have no problem being seen alone in the garden with a gentleman."

She grabbed his sleeve and tugged it, forcing him to lean closer. A waft of orange blossom tickled his nose, the scent sweet and refreshing. "I think we have already established I am not Caroline. What if someone else sees through my disguise?"

"The only way that's going to happen is if you continue to grumble and complain. Hold your head up and walk like you're desperate to be alone with me."

What if he tries to kiss me?

Her silent question bounded back and forth in his head. It was the first coherent thought he'd been able to hone in on. "Don't worry. I'm not about to press myself upon your innocent lips," he added, although he was tempted to see if she tasted as good as he imagined.

"I did not presume you would. But perhaps they are not so innocent."

"Of course not," he said, suppressing a grin. He'd bet fifty guineas she'd turn into a quivering wreck at the mere mention of anything more salacious than kissing.

He liked the way she puckered her lips when annoyed. It made a change from the sultry smiles and provocative pouts usually cast his way. When she'd squared her shoulders, she'd offered him another little treat. *Little* was hardly the right word to describe such a plentiful display. They were soft, heavy and utterly magnificent.

"Are we to stand here all night gaping?" she said, and he shook his head in a bid to focus. "People are beginning to stare."

Elliot glanced over her shoulder to find a sea of sparkling masks quickly averted. "No doubt the gossips are hanging on our every word. I suggest we move outside before we find ourselves depicted as ridiculous caricatures in the newspaper."

He took her hand and tucked it into the crook of his arm before escorting her out onto the terrace and down the three small steps leading to the lawn.

"There's no need to sneak off in search of a secluded spot," he continued. Self-preservation was his only motive. He had no desire to fumble around with an innocent. This creature possessed such a sweet, beguiling charm even the Devil would question which side he was on. "We'll just stroll around the perimeter. I do have my own reputation to consider after all."

She scoffed. "From what I hear, it's a bit late to worry about that."

Somewhere, in a cobwebbed corner of his mind, he felt a stirring of disappointment. Why he should care what she thought of him was a complete mystery. After tonight, he'd probably never set eyes on her again. And the memory would slowly fizzle away until he had no recollection of her sumptuous breasts and witty repartee.

"Are you going to tell me who you are?" He glanced at her vibrant hair, at the teasing mole on her cheek. "You're obviously kin to Miss Rosemond as the likeness is uncanny."

"Then you have answered your own question, my lord."

There was a brief moment of silence while he considered her need to be evasive.

"Are we to wander around aimlessly all night, trying to best the other by offering the wittiest quip?" Elliot smiled as he attempted to listen to her thoughts, but his own mind reflected the conflicting emotions of his body: an intense agitation mingled with the potent thrum of desire.

When she sighed, the sound spoke of anguish and sorrow. "You met with Caroline, three nights ago. I would like to know why. What did you speak of?"

Without warning, he stopped and pulled her round to face

him. In her surprise, she sucked in a breath, and his gaze dropped to the creamy swell.

"My private affairs are my own business," he said, forcing his mind away from all libidinous thoughts. "But if it satisfies you, I have not seen Miss Rosemond for more than a week. And even then, we passed nothing more than the odd pleasantry."

"The odd pleasantry?" she repeated. "Are you usually so blasé about your conquests? I have proof you met with her."

Elliot was not in the habit of having his word questioned. Nor did he particularly like her accusatory tone.

"Remove your mask." The blunt words reflected his frustration. "I cannot hold a conversation with you when your face is obscured."

She hesitated before glancing over her shoulder. There were no other guests in the vicinity, and she turned back to him, her fingers trembling as she removed her mask.

In his mind, he'd constructed a mental picture of Caroline Rosemond, expecting to see the same image. But he was mistaken. The similarity was unarguable, yet the face before him held qualities her kin could never hope to possess. She was not what one would call a striking beauty, but her countenance spoke of kindness, warmth and affection. While she exuded innocence, the long lashes that swept her peachy cheeks and the full lips with a pronounced bow suggested an inner passion he felt compelled to pursue.

He could recall no other woman who appeared to be so delicate and so determined at the same time.

"Wh-what proof do you have?" Good God, had he just stuttered?

The lady lifted her chin. "Caroline made a note of her appointments."

"Before the supposed event, I assume?"

"Well, yes. But—"

"Then you have no proof we actually met at all. My brother

has recently married, and I have been occupied this last week with various family engagements. Ask her when you return home. I do not think she'll be best pleased to discover you've stolen her identity with the intention of snooping into her affairs."

A pang of sadness hit him in the chest—her pain not his own.

"I … I have not seen her for days," she suddenly blurted. "She went out to meet with you and did not return."

Elliot narrowed his gaze. "Surely you don't think I've got anything to do with it. I told you. I have no idea what you're talking about."

She sniffed and sucked in a breath. "I do not know what to think. But when you noticed me and assumed I was Caroline, then I knew you were not responsible for her murder."

"Murder! Why on earth would you think she's been murdered? She's probably been whisked away to Brighton by a lover and simply forgotten to mention the fact."

"You're wrong." She shook her head vigorously, and a stray tendril brushed her cheek. "She invited me to stay because I believe she had something important to tell me. She would never go away and leave me here alone."

In his cynical experience, women like Caroline Rosemond cared only for their own interests. She would bow to the whims of whichever gentleman paid her rent.

"Do you have access to this note?" If something truly had happened to Miss Rosemond, he did not wish to be embroiled in a scandal.

Struggling to meet his gaze, she glanced down as the apples of her cheeks flushed pink. "It is not a note. It … it was written in her diary."

In the four years that he had lived with his affliction, in the years where he had hardened his heart to all sentiment, he had never felt a stirring of emotion in his chest. Yet the look of guilt etched on her face, the way her mouth curled down with remorse, touched him.

Spending so much time with Alexander and Evelyn had evidently softened his steely resolve.

"In times of trouble, we must do what is necessary to find the answers we seek," he said in a bid to console her.

When her tempting lips curled up into a weak smile in response, he suddenly felt like the richest of men.

"That was how I knew you had been on … on intimate terms with her."

"Trust me," he said with a snort. "I have never been on intimate terms with Miss Rosemond."

"But she mentioned your name. When you said you knew her, your words implied otherwise."

"I knew you were not who you were pretending to be. As I said, my intention was to shock so you would stumble."

She gave a resigned nod. "Oh, I see."

"I cannot explain why she saw fit to write such things, but I can assure you I am not a man who welcomes such complications."

"My sister certainly would be a complication in any gentleman's life." She sighed deeply. "I don't know where to turn now. I don't know what to do."

The urge to come to her aid pushed to the fore, but he ignored it. He could not afford to draw undue attention to himself. Perhaps if there was an incentive he might reconsider. What would he give to sate the desire simmering beneath the surface? But despite the clawing need in his loins, he refused to dally with an innocent.

"What about family, can they not help you?"

"Oh, no!" Her eyes grew wide, the soft delicate blue reminding him of a cloudless sky on a summer's afternoon. A wave of regret swept over him, a reminder of all he'd lost, and he sucked in a breath to eradicate the feeling. "There are too many secrets," she continued, "things my mother would not understand."

"I see." She did not need to say any more, and he did not

want to ask. Not out of politeness, but because he did not wish to deepen their acquaintance.

"Well, there is another possibility to explore," she said. "And I would trouble you for just one more thing."

He almost said *anything* but curbed his eager tongue and merely nodded.

"My sister was friendly with a gentleman called Barrington. I would ask you to point him out to me."

"Lord Barrington!" The lady would do well to stay clear of such a man. "I do not know what you intend to do here, but I suggest you let me escort you to my carriage. My coachman will take you wherever you need to go. I am confident your sister will make a dramatic appearance in a day or two. It would not be wise to jeopardise your own reputation."

She gave him a tender smile that expressed gratitude. "I thank you for your counsel. But instinct tells me you're wrong. I know something awful has happened. Just as I know you speak the truth when you proclaim your innocence." Her gaze drifted over his face, and his heart lurched. "Now, can you tell me if you've seen Lord Barrington this evening?"

"Miss Rosemond," he said with a sigh.

"It is Mrs. Denton. Grace Denton. But I ask that you mention it to no one."

"You're married?" Disappointment flooded his chest. The lady looked no older than twenty. While her words revealed a level of maturity and intelligence, there was something pure and unworldly about her. She held an innocence and a level of naivete he found endearing.

She offered a weak smile. "I am a widow."

The revelation caused another momentary surge of emotion. The more they conversed, the deeper, the more intimate his knowledge of her grew. As he tried to shake the feeling of comfortable familiarity, he glanced over her shoulder to see Lord Barrington hovering on the steps as he scoured the garden.

What Elliot did next was unarguably the most foolish, most surprising thing he had ever done. He wrapped his hands around Mrs. Denton's delectable arms, pulled her closer to his needy body and kissed her.

It was a way of preventing her seeking out Barrington, a way to let Barrington know he'd staked his claim. After all, widows were fair game. But when she gasped as her lips touched his, he couldn't fight the urge to plunder her mouth. Wild and reckless, he thrust his tongue deep inside, desperate to taste her, desperate to sate the passion burning within.

Oh, how he wanted to feel disappointed. He wanted to prove that she was just an ordinary woman, nothing special. He wanted her to react as all the others had done: unrefined, vulgar, wanton —the only sort of woman he deserved.

But the Lord had delivered his most virtuous, most tempting angel to torment him.

With surprising strength, Mrs. Denton pushed him away. She swallowed visibly as her breathing came short and quick, her soft breasts heaving to punish him all the more. Bringing her gloved hand to her lips, she touched the tips of her fingers to her mouth.

"Mrs. Denton—" he began, but he had no words to account for his actions.

The situation was foreign to him. The more he thought, the more his mind grew hazy, which was why he failed to notice her draw back her hand. When it connected with his cheek, it sounded like a dull thud but stung his pride like the lash of a whip.

"You mistake me for someone else, my lord," she said, kindness and warmth replaced with coldness and loathing.

The stone barricade around his heart shook. Bits of broken mortar crumbled away. God help him, he wanted her more than ever—to see her smile, to trust him, to open her caring heart to him.

Damn it.

Sensing her disappointment and disdain, he stepped back. “Go.” The word came out as a growl, a vicious warning and he simply stared as she pulled down her mask, picked up her skirt and ran off into the night.

CHAPTER 3

Grace raced through the garden, desperate to be away from the world of sin and degradation her sister found so appealing. Inside, her chest burned. Days of suppressed emotion refused to be tempered. Still, she fought to keep it at bay.

To cry would mean failure and she would not desert her sister in her hour of need.

Lord Markham proved to be worthy of his scandalous reputation. Of course, she'd only had the word of a stranger and a few notes in a diary, but his crude assault supported their statements.

A pang of sadness filled her heart.

Not just for her poor sister. During her conversation with Lord Markham, she had glimpsed a kind and considerate man. She had confided in him, talked to him as a friend and he had treated her like a common harlot. When she returned home, she would study the diary, convinced she must have missed something. As despite his dissipated antics, she believed the reckless lord's protestations of innocence.

Finding no exit out of the garden and reluctant to step back into the ballroom, Grace made her way down a flight of stone steps leading to the basement door. Moving through the servants' quarters, she followed the corridor up to a service entrance and soon found herself out on the street.

Without a cape for protection from the chilly night air and no money to hire a hackney, she hurried along the pavement before coming to an abrupt halt at the crossroads.

With nothing to assist her but the muted light from the lamps, she scoured the streets looking for a familiar sign or building. Nothing captured her attention. Was it left and then right or the other way around? It had all seemed so simple earlier in the evening. She had been so desperate to get to the masquerade she'd forgotten to make a mental note of the directions.

Mrs. Whitman would have a fit of the vapours if she could see her now.

What sort of lady roams the streets alone at night, she would say, dressed as though she's eager to be tupped at the back of the buttery? Only a naive fool intent on courting trouble.

Hearing raucous laughter spilling out onto the street behind her, she made the quick decision to turn left. She'd only taken a dozen steps when she heard the clip of heels charging along behind her. With her heart stuck in her throat and feeling a strange sense of foreboding, she picked up her skirt and ran.

"Caroline." The frustrated masculine voice called out to her. "Caroline. Wait. I only want to talk."

She didn't want to wait.

She didn't want to talk.

Fear gripped her again. She wished she could close her eyes and wake up miles from this dreadful place.

The clicking got closer, the culprit's shoes striking the ground with efficient regularity. In the dark, she didn't notice the uneven stone. The loose-fitting gloves provided little protection as she lost her balance and tumbled to the ground. The pain of stubbing her toe was nothing compared to the burning sensation searing her forearms as she slid along the cold slabs.

It took a few seconds for her mind to catch up with her body. But when the large hand grabbed her wrist to pull her up, she cried out in pain as the determined fingers dug into the grazed skin.

"You're hurting me."

"Why are you running from me?" the gentleman said. Ignoring her plea, he swung her around to face him. "I just want to talk to you. I waited for over an hour at the theatre."

So this was Lord Barrington.

Dressed as an Elizabethan courtier with his white stockings and thick ruff, he towered above her. She felt weak and minuscule in comparison. The grey flecks in his side-whiskers and the prominent lines framing his thin mouth suggested the man was much older than Caroline.

"I must go home," she said, almost losing her gloves as she tried to pull away from his grasp. But he took hold of her hands and refused to let them go.

"Look what you've done." He turned her arms over to reveal the thick pink welts flecked with blood. The ripped lace frill at one elbow dangled loosely. "Why won't you let me take care of you?"

"Please, just let me go. We can talk tomorrow. I need to apply some ointment to the wounds, and it's—"

"You said you would consider my proposal. You said you would give me your answer." He was still panting from overexertion. His sickly sweet breath forced her to turn her head away to inhale. "I do not appreciate being made a fool of."

In theory, his words should have soothed her. Lord Barrington believed he was speaking to Caroline and evidently knew nothing of her disappearance. Yet his eyes held a wild, urgent look as though she were a juicy piece of pie and he couldn't wait to satisfy his slavering chops.

"I … I don't have an answer for you."

"Is it the terms? Do you wish to negotiate?"

Negotiate? He was not buying a horse or items of equipage. "I need more time."

"You'll give me your answer now," he growled, jerking her closer. "I cannot spend another night wondering if I'll have you."

Panic flared.

She had no idea what this man was capable of.

With a quick glance left and right, the street appeared deserted. But a blanket of fog had descended, the roads ahead disappearing into a blurry haze. If she could run, if she could get a good start, she might lose him.

Grace tried to tug her hands from his grasp. "At least let me remove my mask so we can talk."

Her words seemed to placate him, and he let go of her hands. As she removed her mask, she swiped him across the face with it, ignoring his blasphemous curse as she rushed towards the cloud-like mass. But his strides were longer, his obsession fuelling his determination, and he grabbed the back of her dress and pulled her back against his chest. She felt the material strain in protest, heard the delicate threads tear apart.

"I'm taking you home," he said, his tone harsh, unyielding. "You'll not run away from me again."

The sound of carriage wheels rattling over the cobbles caught her attention, and she cried for help as it drew up alongside them. Lord Barrington smothered her mouth with his hand, his arm securing her tight to his body. Grace heard a door open, a gruff command and the dull thud of someone jumping down to the pavement.

"Get your bloody hands off her."

Lord Barrington fell back, pulling her down with him. As he released his grip to shield his face from a barrage of punches, she scurried away, coming to stand near the carriage door.

Despite being a good few inches shorter, Lord Markham delivered a spectacular display of fighting finesse. Dodging Barrington's clumsy fists, he returned with short, sharp blows to his stomach. Bouncing lightly on the balls of his feet, he dealt Barrington a jab to his jaw causing the man to sag to the ground.

Lord Markham glanced over his shoulder and nodded towards the carriage. "Get in."

His eyes appeared darker, dangerously sinister, his voice a little hoarse. He did not need to tell her a second time. As she fell back into the red leather seat, her heart beating so erratically she could hardly catch her breath, she heard Lord Markham telling Barrington to forget what he had seen. It seemed a rather odd thing to say. Even odder was his need to repeat the words over and over again.

Lord Markham yelled to his coachman, climbed inside the carriage and slammed the door before dropping into the seat opposite. As they rumbled along, his ragged breathing penetrated the silence. Tension thrummed in the air. Intermittent rays of light from the passing streetlamps licked at his irises. They were no longer dark but a bright, vibrant green.

She watched him slide his tongue over his teeth, no doubt to curb his temper or to prevent him from saying something he may regret. A shiver ran through her body in anticipation.

"Here," he said, shrugging out of his coat. "You're trembling. And your dress is torn." He shuffled to the edge of his seat, leant forward and draped it around her shoulders.

Grace stared at him. She resisted the urge to inhale deeply as she caught the familiar scent of sandalwood. The warmth of the garment relaxed her a little, and she pulled it tighter across her chest.

"Thank you for stopping. I … I don't know where I would be if you'd not seen me … if you had just driven by without a care."

He threw himself forward. The shock made her jump. "I'll tell you where you'd be." His breath came quick as anger burst forth. "You'd be in Barrington's carriage. He would have taken you regardless of your protests." Throwing himself back in the seat, he brushed his hands through his ebony locks and exhaled. "What were you thinking?"

"Nothing. When I left the garden after you … well, I decided to go home." She snuggled into his coat as if it were strong masculine arms enveloping her. "I didn't know Barrington had followed me."

Her explanation did not appear to soften his mood. With a scowl, he removed his gloves and flexed his fingers while examining his hands.

"Where do you live?" he growled.

"Cobham."

He gave a frustrated sigh. "I mean where in London are you staying?"

"I came to stay with Caroline."

"Unlike most men, I have no idea where that is."

His words roused her anger. When he spoke of her sister, he did not bother to hide his contempt, and it hurt. "Your opinion of my sister's character is yours to own. But I do not wish to sit here and listen to your cutting remarks whenever I mention her name. Despite her mistakes, I love her and each jibe is like a knife to my heart."

He was silent for the longest time, yet she felt his intense gaze roam over her body like nimble fingers. "Are you always so open and honest with your emotions?"

Usually, she kept most things to herself. Sharing one's life and one's bed with a man whose heart belonged to another blurred the lines between lies and truth. The three short months she'd spent as Henry's wife equated to nothing more than a tiny fragment of her life. That thought made it easier to bear.

"I'm honest when the need arises." She decided not to say any more. To be truly honest would mean telling him she found him easy to talk to. He was intelligent and logical, even if his lascivious ways influenced his actions.

"Then I shall do the same," he said, arrogance replacing his anger. "You cannot return to Miss Rosemond's house."

Grace sat bolt upright. "What do you mean? I have nowhere else to go."

"Barrington will seek you out. He is renowned for his obsessions and in his warped mind he won't believe you're not Caroline. He will assume you're using it as an excuse to refuse him."

"But I can't go home, not to Cobham, not without news of Caroline." She swallowed deeply, trying to ease the tightening sensation in her throat. The thought of her waking up to find Barrington peering down at her in bed made her feel nauseous.

"What choice do you have? There is no other option open to you," he said, but his tone lacked conviction.

Grace shook her head. "I can't go home."

"You should not be embroiled in all of this." His words revealed a hint of frustration. "You're obviously a good person, kind and loyal to a fault."

She had been called many things: dull, weak, spiritless. No gentleman had ever complimented her character. She felt a flush rise to her cheeks. Her gaze drifted over his firm jaw, over his soft lips and sinful green eyes. The fluttering in her stomach felt strange, yet oddly exciting, something she had never experienced with Henry.

But she did not need these sorts of complications—she needed something else from him.

"Have you ever met someone for the first time and felt an unusual connection?" she said. "As though you've known them your whole life yet you've only known them less than a day?"

He gave an amused snort. "And then there are people you've known your entire life who still feel like strangers."

"Exactly." She smiled at his response as it confirmed her theory. He had a good heart beneath the bravado. "I need your help. I need a friend, my lord, someone to trust."

"You mean you need someone to help you find Miss Rosemond."

"Just for a few days," she said, pleading her case. "I know it's unheard of, unacceptable even. A man and woman cannot be friends without someone suggesting impropriety. But no one need know you're assisting me. No one knows me here in town. Besides, if anyone should see us together they will assume I'm Caroline."

"I can't help you," he said, shaking his head. "I am a complicated man and not always good company."

"You mean you've never been friends with a woman."

"I fear the time has arisen for me to be honest. I ask your forgiveness in advance should my words offend."

"Say what you will," she said. "There is no one here to stand in judgement."

"Very well." He sighed, sat back and folded his arms. "I have only one type of relationship with women, and it involves little to no conversation. Intimacy is something I avoid on all levels, with everyone."

"Yet here you are in a closed carriage, telling me something you've never told another."

"Well … I …"

He couldn't answer. How wonderful.

"I understand," she said. "And I would never want you to do anything that would make you feel uncomfortable." She glanced out of the window. Despite the fog, she still had no idea where she was. "Arlington Street, if you please."

"Pardon?"

"You may drop me on the corner of Arlington Street." Grace pulled his coat from around her shoulders and placed it on the seat next to her. "And thank you for the use of your coat."

"Miss Rosemond lives on Arlington Street?"

Studying his wide-eyed expression, she said, "Why? What's wrong with that?"

"It is a stone's throw from three of the most popular gentlemen's clubs. You can't stay there."

For a man who had obviously indulged in many lascivious liaisons, he was very stuffy. "But I have spent the last two days there on my own."

His gaze drifted leisurely down to the topaz necklace, dipping lower still. "Damn," he whispered, and then gave an exasperated sigh. "Look. I may know of somewhere you can go. I'm not making any promises, but my brother and his wife are staying with her aunt, and she is sailing for India in the morning. Perhaps you may stay there for a few days."

Grace clapped her hands together as a feeling of hope flooded her chest. "It sounds perfect. I'm sure I'll be fine on my own tonight."

"Tonight?"

"Her aunt leaves in the morning you said. I'm sure you've given Lord Barrington a dreadful fright and—"

"What makes you say that?" He sounded curious, yet defensive and again it struck her as odd.

"You pummelled the man to a pulp. He's probably gone home to lick his wounds and nurse his injured pride."

"I wouldn't count on it. I told you, the gentleman is obsessed with Caroline Rosemond. Everyone's talking about it. I'll drop you at Arlington Street while you collect a few things. Tonight, I'm afraid you will have to come home with me."

CHAPTER 4

The words had left his mouth before the logical part of his brain dismissed the idea as ludicrous. But what other choice was there? If he had not noticed Barrington racing down the street, heaven only knows what would have happened to Grace Denton.

The lady was a menace unto herself. She appeared to have no concept of how dangerous the city could be for a young woman on her own. Parading around in such a state of dishabille, she'd have been lucky to make it down the length of James' Street without one young buck trying his chances.

Bloody hell.

He still couldn't believe he had agreed to help her.

Elliot glanced across at the woman who roused his ire as much as his desire and realised the carriage had stopped.

"It's a little further down, number twelve, but I'll walk from here." She sounded more confident now, as though she'd had a complete memory lapse and couldn't possibly be the woman who had just been attacked in the street.

As her hand settled on the door handle, he noticed the raw pink scar peeking out of the top of her glove. The area was littered with spots of dried blood, and he took a deep breath before taking her hand and turning it over.

"What's happened here?" He tried to curb his temper, tried to curb the sweet fire heating his blood at the mere touch of her hand. Thank goodness he'd never get the opportunity to lie with her, to cover her naked body with his own. There'd be nothing left of him but a sooty pile of charcoaled remains.

"I tripped and fell when Barrington chased me. It's nothing. It's just a little unsightly."

Nothing? She'd been injured whilst fleeing a madman. Anger bubbled away inside, and he glanced out of the window. Heaven knows how many gentlemen knew where Caroline Rosemond lived.

"You're not going in there on your own." He was starting to sound like one of the domineering patriarchs he despised and detested. "I'm coming in with you."

When they entered the hall, he'd not expected to find it so quiet, so cold and still. "Where are the servants?" he said, opening a door off the hall and peering into the darkness.

"Caroline only had a maid and a cook. I've not seen them for two days, either." She chuckled to herself. "Hence, the mess I made with my hair."

Loose tendrils hung about her cheeks and dangled down her back. He liked the wild and unruly style. It was natural and unassuming, just like everything else about her.

He walked over to her. "You have been here alone for two days?"

When she nodded he had a sudden urge to ease her fears, to make everything right so she need never worry again.

"That's why I came to the masquerade," she said. "I rifled through Caroline's invitations until I found something suitable. I was desperate. You see, Mrs. Whitman is to call for me next week on her way back to Cobham."

"I assume this Mrs. Whitman has no idea she left you in the incapable hands of a courtesan?"

"Of course not. My mother believes my sister's a paid companion to an elderly matron. That's one of the reasons Caroline came to London."

Every courtesan had a tale to tell. Some chose wealth over integrity. Some chose a life of immorality over a life in the workhouse. But, judging by her sister's sweet temperament, he guessed Caroline Rosemond's story involved an unsolicited encounter with a scoundrel. He would wager a hundred guineas the elderly matron had a rake for a grandson.

A frisson of fear rushed through him when he imagined Grace Denton struggling against a man twice her size. Regardless of his own concerns, he would help her find her sister and see her safely out of London, back to the sleepy village of Cobham.

It was the only scenario his conscience would allow.

"You can tell me more about it later," he said, feeling a desperate need to drink. "Once I've checked the upper rooms, you may gather your things, and we'll be on our way."

He mounted the stairs two at a time, aware of her racing up behind him. "I'll come up with you. It feels strange being here alone in the dark."

"Come, show me your room," he said, waiting for her to catch up.

"It's that one." She pointed through a gap in the balusters to the door at the end of the landing.

With some hesitation, Elliot prised the door from the jamb and entered first. He checked under the bed and inside the armoire, paranoia being a feeling foreign to him until now. But it distracted his mind from the thought of being alone with the pretty widow in her bedchamber. It did not prevent his cock from stirring. After all, he was a man, not a bloody saint.

"There are no candles," she said. "I used the last one and couldn't find any more. I'll just change my clothes. I can come back for the rest tomorrow."

"I'll help you collect what you need, so there's no reason to return." The last thing he wanted was to rummage around in a drawer full of the lady's undergarments, but he'd be damned if he'd let her come back alone. And with his aversion to sunlight, he could not leave the house until dark.

Damn it. In his eagerness to play the noble hero, he had not considered the restrictions of his affliction.

Mrs. Denton threw her gloves onto the bed, removed a dress from the armoire and held it up to the window before taking it behind the dressing screen. "This will do for a day or two," she said.

He found he could not form a reply. His mind was engaged in imagining the soft curve of her hips, the peachy-cream skin he knew would feel like silk to the touch. When she draped the torn medieval gown over the screen, he almost groaned out loud, and he breathed a sigh of relief when she walked out wearing the pale blue gown.

"I hate to inconvenience you further," she continued, "but would you mind if I took a bath?"

"What, here?" Surely she didn't expect him to traipse up and down the stairs carrying buckets of water.

"No," she said, removing a few items of clothing from the drawers. "Later, when I come home with you."

Such innocent words spoke of deep intimacy. Panic flared. He felt out of his depth, floundering amidst a sea of turbulent emotions. He'd never taken a lady to his home. Since his tenth birthday, the day his mother left and disappeared without a trace, he swore never to allow another woman into his place of sanctuary—let alone bathe in his blasted tub.

Damn, he only had male staff.

"I'm sure it won't be a problem," he said stiffly, trying to banish the image of her lounging naked in the copper vessel. Reining in his errant thoughts, he stepped closer while she piled some items into his arms. "You'll need a brush," he said, "and don't forget the diary. We can study it together. I'm rather curious to see what she's written about me."

The lady gasped. "The diary. I almost forgot." Scurrying over to the dressing table, she dropped to her knees and ducked underneath. Even in the dark, she offered him a splendid view, ripe and round, as she grumbled and mumbled to herself before shuffling out. "I thought it best to hide it," she said, clutching the box under her arm as she brushed the dust from her dress.

Elliot didn't ask any questions. He was desperate to get home. He needed something to soothe the raging fire in his belly. Hopefully, the smooth red liquid would slide easily down his throat to calm the restless feeling consuming him.

When they reached Portman Square, Elliot helped her inside with her things. After a brief conversation with Whithers, whose mouth hung open for so long Elliot feared it would never close properly again, they retired to the study while a room was prepared.

"Do you mind if I sit?" she said, gesturing to the chair next to the fire.

"Please, make yourself at home." It was only for a night, he told himself, as the words left his lips. In an hour she would be tucked up in bed. By the time he ventured down tomorrow evening, she would be ready to depart.

He watched her warm her hands by the fire, saw her flinch as the heat aggravated the grazed skin. "Let me put something on those cuts. It will take down the swelling, soften the skin so it won't feel as tight."

"That would be wonderful." She examined the marks as she sat down. "I've tried to forget about it, but it's still a little sore."

Elliot took a glass and poured a small amount of brandy into the bottom. Walking over to his desk, he opened the drawer, removed a handkerchief and a flask of laudanum and pretended to add a few drops.

Swirling the amber liquid in the glass, he came to sit opposite her. "Give me your hand." He felt oddly nervous, as though he'd only recently progressed from the school room and being in the presence of a woman was a stimulating enough experience in itself.

Mrs. Denton's gaze drifted over his face, and she glanced down at his open palm before placing her hand tentatively in his.

A host of overwhelming sensations flooded his body. He could feel the pulse of her heart beating against his skin. A strange tingling sensation made him feel weightless, somewhat dizzy. His gaze met hers and he noticed her bottom lip trembling.

God, he'd had many women, taken his pleasure in every way possible. Nothing compared to the craving he felt deep in his chest when he looked at her. He shook his head and tried to focus.

"Look away," he said, aware of the slight change in the pitch of his voice. "It will hurt less."

She nodded and turned to look at the flames.

Elliot put the handkerchief to his mouth, wetting a corner before patting the broken skin.

She sucked in a breath as he continued with his delicate ministrations, touching it to his mouth, dabbing the skin. All the while he watched her, aching for something he could not explain.

"What happened to your husband?" He did not mean to pry into her private affairs, but he needed to distract his mind.

"Henry fell off his horse and broke his neck."

There was something cold and detached about her reply and her hand remained steady in his. It told him all he needed to know but still he said, "It must have been awful for you."

"Only awful because a man lost his life being reckless." She sighed deeply and turned to look at him. "Sorry. I should not have said that."

Her gaze held his for a moment, and he saw pain reflected there, perhaps even disappointment.

Placing her hand gently in her lap, he reached for her other hand, and she turned away as he dabbed at the dried specks of blood.

"What I mean to say is we were only married for a few months."

Elliot could feel her sadness surrounding him, pressing down on his shoulders like a heavy weight. Sadness for what? he thought. She had more or less admitted to feeling nothing for the man whose name she bore.

Driven by a compulsion to discover more, he asked, "There was no love between you?"

"Love?" she echoed giving a cynical snort. "No, there was no love, only resentment." She turned to face him again. "Have you ever been in love?"

The question hit him like a blow to the chest. For a man who avoided intimacy, it was far too intrusive. But he had set this scene, provoked her to open her heart and so she deserved to hear his answer.

"No. I have never been in love. I do not believe there is such a thing." Indeed, his mother had taught him that. Even so, spending time with Alexander and Evelyn had caused him to doubt his own philosophy. "All human actions are motivated by selfishness in one form or another. The great poets would have us believe love is an exotic destination, the reward for surviving a long and perilous voyage. I'm more inclined to agree with the notion that it is a form of manipulation. Where the weak-minded become slaves to their passion and dress it all up as something far more profound."

"I'm not sure I agree," she said, glancing down at his hand wrapped around hers. "While experience tells me you may be right, I would prefer to think of love as a feeling of deep affection. To be cherished and accepted for who you are must surely be the greatest gift imaginable."

"I have heard fanciful tales of such things, yet in all my thirty years I have only ever witnessed it once."

Rather than appear discouraged, she simply smiled. "Then there is hope, is there not?"

Since the night he'd been turned by a devil, *hope* was a word obliterated from his vocabulary.

"There," he said, letting go of her hand, desperate to put an end to the conversation. "It will still be sore but will heal much more quickly. You should notice a difference come morning."

She glanced down and examined both arms. "It feels better already. You must tell me how to make the tincture."

He stood and walked over to the drinks tray, swallowing the brandy in one mouthful when she wasn't looking. With desperate eyes, he pulled the stopper from the decanter of blood, knowing how the smallest taste would calm him.

"Would you care for some refreshment?"

"Thank you. I'll have a small measure of whatever you're having."

Groaning inwardly, he replaced the stopper and poured them both a glass of brandy.

Picking up the diary from the small table next to her, she flicked through to the relevant page. "Here it is. The comment about her appointment to meet with you."

"Would you mind if I examined her note?" he said, swapping the diary for the glass of brandy.

He took the book over to the desk and angled the candle to study the script.

She came to stand beside him and peered over his shoulder. "You see." She pointed to his name, her arm brushing against his. "It looks like Markham."

With all the will in the world, he couldn't concentrate while she was standing so closely. She was a widow ripe for the plucking. As she turned the page and mumbled something about the way his name was written, all he could think of was her spread out over the wooden surface, his hands grabbing her waist as he positioned himself between long luscious legs.

"You're staring at it blankly," she said. "Can you not see

what I mean? I don't know why I've never noticed it before. Perhaps because I have only ever studied it in the daylight."

"Sorry, what have you not noticed before?"

She tutted. "The dot."

"The dot?" he repeated.

"You've not been listening to a word I have said. The next page is blank, but if you examine it under the light, you can see the indentations. It isn't Markham. It is Mark dot ham."

Elliot turned the page to study it himself. "I see what you mean. So you think she met with someone called Mark?"

"I'm not sure," she said with a sigh. "Your name is mentioned, which is why I assumed it was you. But there is no other mention of a Mark."

Curious to know what Miss Rosemond had written, he flicked back through the pages. "Where are the notes she made about me?"

She snatched the diary from him. "It is rude to read someone's private thoughts. I only did so because I feared the worst." She studied his face for a moment, sighed and then conceded. "Under the circumstances, I suppose you deserve to know what she wrote, but I shall read it to you."

"Very well."

Finding the relevant page, she began. "Lord Markham was as arrogant as ever, but I see the way he looks at me with those lustful eyes. Given time, I believe I have what it takes to win him over. The only qualities he admires amount to—" She stopped abruptly.

"Go on."

"The rest doesn't really matter."

"It matters to me. Go on."

"The … the only qualities he admires amount to nothing more than a m-moist mouth and a warm body. But I believe the latter is somewhat negotiable."

Disdain bubbled away in his gut, and he stormed over to the drinks table. The blood slithered into the glass without making a sound. He swallowed it down, closed his eyes and savoured the taste. Truth be told, he felt ashamed. Something he'd never felt, something he never expected he would.

Mrs. Denton walked over to him. "It is just one person's opinion."

"Is it? I wouldn't be so sure."

What troubled him most was why he wanted Grace Denton to think better of him. Why did the idea of finding something more than the shallow, insipid women he was used to cause hope to unfurl like the first fresh flower of spring?

A knock on the door disturbed his reverie, and he glanced up to see Whithers.

"The guest room is ready, my lord, and a bath has been drawn."

"Thank you, Whithers. You may leave the tub in the room tonight and dispense with it in the morning."

Whithers coughed into his fist. "And Lord Hartford is here."

What the hell did Leo want? At this hour, he was usually nestled comfortably between soft thighs.

Mrs. Denton stepped forward. "Invite your guest in, my lord. I'm tired and shall retreat to my room."

It was for the best. The more time he spent in her company, the more he lost all grip on reality, the more his mind was plagued by whimsical fantasies.

"Give us a minute, Whithers, and then you may show Lord Hartford in." As Whithers retreated, Elliot turned to his delectable guest. "I'm a late riser, so we will confer later in the afternoon. Whithers will provide anything you need in the meantime."

She smiled, but the beautiful image faded as Leo's voice boomed through the hall. "Is he in here?" The gentleman strode in like a true Turkish prince. "As you left the party so early, I thought I'd bring it to you. The ladies are waiting in my carriage and—" He stopped abruptly, his wide eyes focusing on Grace Denton.

"Forgive me," Leo said, offering a gracious bow. "I did not expect you to have company."

Elliot turned to Mrs. Denton. "Whithers will show you up to your room."

She inclined her head. "Thank you, my lord."

Ignoring Leo's frown, he watched her walk from the room.

"You have brought a woman into your home?" Leo whispered. "I thought you said women like Caroline Rosemond were not worth the effort."

Faced with the dilemma of telling Leo the truth, Elliot said, "Can you do something for me?"

Leo appeared surprised by the question. "Of course. You do not need to ask."

"If I write a note, will you take it to Alexander? I need Evelyn's help."

"Certainly. I take it you're not coming with me. The delights waiting in my carriage are no match for the skill of a seasoned courtesan."

Elliot glanced up at the ceiling, imagined a bathing scene unfolding. "What I have here is something far superior than even I can comprehend."

CHAPTER 5

Grace squinted against the brightness of the morning sun as she peered out through the heavy drapes. People were milling about outside. A milkmaid cried her wares in the square as she swung her pails on a yoke. A sweeper continued the fruitless task of clearing the street, a carriage disturbing his ministrations as it rattled past.

No one had called to wake her. Not even the smallest sliver of light had penetrated the darkness. The absence of any scrumptious smells wafting up from the kitchen led her to believe she'd slept through breakfast.

Finding a clock on the mantel, she noted it was almost nine. Grace kept to country hours and never slept past seven. But it must have been well into the early hours when she finally stumbled into bed.

Recalling Lord Markham's fondness for rising late, she assumed it would be at least three hours before he made an appearance. It didn't seem quite right to be wandering around his house with him being absent.

Dressing quickly, she pulled the cord and waited for the maid. Responding to the light tap on her door, Grace was surprised to find a footman enter her chamber.

"Could you have a maid bring fresh water? And perhaps some toast and tea as I fear I've missed breakfast."

The footman inclined his head. "There are no maids, madam. Lord Markham keeps a small select staff. I will provide for your needs."

How odd. She had never heard of such a prestigious house having no maids. What about the beds and the laundry?

"Will you be taking breakfast in your room, madam, or shall I set a place in the dining room?" Noting her hesitation, the footman added, "Here, mealtimes are rather informal affairs."

Grace smiled. She found Lord Markham's unconventional habits quite refreshing. The gentleman conveyed an air of mysteriousness. His dark, brooding features implied a volatile, unpredictable temperament. Yet he had been far more considerate and attentive to her needs than she could have ever expected.

"Then I shall take my breakfast in here," she replied, feeling a little more at ease.

When the footman left, she jumped back onto the huge bed and grabbed the diary from the nightstand. The grazes to her arms were still visible, though they had healed remarkably well overnight and caused not the slightest irritation.

The footman returned with a pitcher of clean water and two empty buckets and asked if Grace minded if he cleared away the bathtub. Some twenty minutes later, he returned with the breakfast tray, and she was finally able to concentrate on her task.

In the last two days, she'd scoured the notes looking for any indication as to where her sister may have gone. Perhaps starting at the beginning was not the best idea. Only last night, they had made an interesting discovery on the last page. Grace stared at the dot again as she bit into her toast. Had it not been for the indentation on the blank page she might have missed it.

Her sister wrote with a heavy hand, and so she ran the pad of her finger gently over the surface of the empty page in the hope of feeling any other marks pressed into the paper. The texture felt different near the bottom. To the naked eye, it was almost impossible to see anything.

Then she had an idea.

Rushing over to the fireplace, she rubbed her finger along the inside of the chimney-breast and smudged the soot over the marks on the blank page. Like a conjurer's trick, the words appeared before her eyes, practically rising off the page.

Caroline must have used the diary to lean on when she had written a note as there were no torn or missing pages. Grace could make out a string of words, nothing more. What she did see caused a sudden burst of panic.

I'm tired of the games and the lies ... I want to end it all.

Grace struggled to catch her breath and her pounding heart felt ready to burst from her chest. Tears threatened to fall. Just spending one day as Caroline Rosemond had proved a horrendous ordeal. She gathered the diary to her chest and hugged it tight. If only Caroline would have confided in her.

Not knowing what to do. Not knowing what to think. She wished Lord Markham was awake. She needed to talk to him. He would know what to say to calm her. He'd apply his usual logical approach to the situation, and she'd be able to breathe freely again.

Pacing the floor for what felt like hours, she glanced at the mantel clock again. Surely it was later than eleven. Perhaps she should tap on his door. Given the severity of the information she had uncovered, it was unlikely he would mind.

Tucking the diary under her arm, she opened the chamber door and wandered to the other end of the landing. If she heard a sound coming from one of the rooms, she would know he was awake.

But she could hardly storm into a gentleman's bedchamber. Heaven knows what sight would greet her.

The thought caused her cheeks to flame.

For goodness' sake, she was hardly a young girl making her debut. She had an intimate knowledge of men, even if her experience was limited to one man in particular. To one cold-hearted devil.

There were four other doors situated on the landing. Grace imagined Lord Markham would want a room overlooking the garden: a quieter, more subdued space. That left two options. She was drawn to the room furthest from her own. With no female staff in the house, she guessed the lascivious nature of the man she'd grown to like demanded her room be at opposite ends of the house from his own.

She tapped lightly on the door she suspected was his, but he did not answer. Grace gave an indiscreet cough and then knocked again.

Nothing.

Oh, well. Her poor heart would give out if she had to wait a moment longer and with trembling fingers, she wrapped her hand around the handle.

Lord Markham was understanding and considerate, and not at all the mean-spirited monster Henry once was. She had nothing to fear.

Elliot knew Grace Denton had entered his chamber without lifting his head from his pillow. He had picked up threads of her thoughts as she hovered outside, assumed she would walk away, convince herself that to enter a gentleman's private chamber was certain folly.

But he should have known it would not be the case. When the lady set her mind to a task, she'd not let something as trivial as impropriety stand in her way. Next time, he'd be sure to turn the key in the lock.

As the door groaned in protest, he snuffed out the candle, laid the book flat on his chest and closed his eyes. If he squinted, he could just see her outline entering the room. With only the briefest hesitation, she padded lightly over to the bed, stood over him and stared.

Her gaze drifted over his bare chest, lingered on the dusting of hair trailing down below his abdomen. With part of his branding mark visible, he wondered what she would make of it. Thank the Lord he'd kept his trousers on, else she'd not be able to mistake the sight of his arousal. The need to have her had consumed him from the first moment he'd met her, more so when he'd heard the evidence of her kind heart and witty tongue. She intrigued him. He was captivated by her contradicting qualities: a deeply passionate nature mingled with a soft, sweet temperament.

"Lord Markham," she whispered. But he knew if he opened his eyes fully, if he gazed upon her sultry smile, the needs of his famished body would overpower all rational thought. And so he tried to keep his breathing calm, more sedate, as he feigned slumber.

She sighed, the sound revealing frustration rather than fatigue.

He felt her move away before he noted the sound of light footsteps. Disappointment and relief waged an internal war. He knew which side he was on. Curiosity forced him to peer through squinted lids, and he choked on the sudden wave of panic exploding from his gut.

"D-don't," he yelled as her hand gripped the drapes.

She jumped as he stumbled from the bed. His arms and legs struggled to keep up with the chaotic train of his thoughts.

"I must speak with you urgently," she said. "It's so dark in here."

"Leave them." The words sounded like an incoherent growl as he tried to reach her before she gave into her innocent whim.

Elliot heard the swishing sound before the slivers of light hit his chest. The piercing rays seared his skin. He put his hands to his face as he crumpled to the floor, shock swallowing down his cries.

"What? What's wrong?" she cried, rushing down to his side.

Amidst the agonising pain, he knew he had to force the words from his lips. "C-close them … close the drapes. Hurry."

With a mix of fear and confusion marring her brow she did as he asked, dragging them across to plunge them back into darkness.

Relief coursed through him.

She knelt down at his side. Her trembling hands hovered over him, patting the air above his chest. "Your skin, it is all blistered and burnt. What can I do?"

"The decanter," he said, his breathing raspy, ragged. He knew his eyes were dark, his teeth visible. Lifting a limp arm, he pointed to the console table on the far side of the room. "I need to drink."

With wide eyes, she gaped at the sharp points overhanging his lip. "Good heavens, what's happening to you?"

"Just … just get me a drink."

She hurried away and came back with the decanter and glass. "Shall I pour it?"

"Help me sit up." His arms felt weak as he tried to prop himself up on his elbows.

Understanding his dilemma, she sat on the floor behind him and pulled him up to lean against her chest, her shoulder supporting his head. She removed the stopper and brought the decanter to his lips.

That first smooth sip of blood brought instant relief. He closed his eyes and exhaled deeply, aware of her other hand stroking his hair from his brow. He could sense her fear, her confusion, but she continued to help him take small sips, continued to soothe his spirit.

"Don't… don't be frightened," he managed to say, aware of her chest heaving as she struggled to breathe.

"Had I not seen it with my own eyes, I could scarcely believe it."

"It is a terrible affliction." He took a large gulp from the decanter. "But beneath it all, I am the same man."

"The drink seems to be helping," she said incredulously. "Your breathing sounds a little better. But you're dribbling."

When she wiped away the trickle of blood with the pad of her finger, a warm feeling flooded his chest. Perhaps assuming it was wine, he heard her suck away the residue, heard her retch at the taste. "What on earth are you drinking?"

Too weak to manipulate her thoughts, too tired to care, he told the truth. "It is blood. My illness demands I drink it."

There, he had said it. He had spoken the words to another. Despite fearing the consequences, he felt the shackles of his burden break in two.

"Blood!" The loud gasp revealed the true depth of her fear.

"I do not drink it out of choice."

"Are … are you dying?"

"No. I am not dying." The parts of him that controlled all feeling and emotion had long ceased to function. "Can you help me up onto the bed?"

Taking the decanter from him and placing it on the floor, she put her hand on his back to support him as she stood, the intimacy of the action overshadowed by necessity. Scooping her arms under his, she helped him up to lie on the bed.

"I need a few minutes to rest. But I will answer any questions you may have."

He expected her to flee the room at the first opportunity, but she came to stand at his side, her gaze roaming over the scars on his chest, up to his sharp teeth, his black eyes.

She shuffled back, just a step or two. "What's wrong with you? Part of me wants to run far from here. Part of me is desperate to know how to help you."

He blinked a few times. "If you want to leave, by all means do so. I only ask that you do not mention what you have witnessed."

When he regained his strength, he would make her forget.

"Did the sunlight do that?" She nodded to the marks on his chest, stretched her fingers out but didn't touch them. "Did the sun burn your skin?"

"The illness causes a severe reaction to sunlight."

Trembling fingers came up to cover her mouth. Was it a means of protection or to suppress shock? He wasn't sure.

"It is not contagious," he added. "You will not catch it."

"Your eyes … they're different."

"I need blood to live. My eyes darken when I feed."

She leant closer and peered into his eyes and he fought the urge to take her in his arms. "They are green again," she said, marvelling at the fact.

Amazed at her response, he said, "Are you not frightened? I want you to tell me the truth." For some strange reason, he needed her to be honest with him.

"Of course, I was frightened," she said. "I thought you were going to die."

"I meant are you not frightened by my monstrous appearance?"

She shrugged. "Yes, but it is hardly monstrous. How long have you suffered from this dreadful illness?"

"Four years." Elliot took a deep breath. "Look, Mrs. Denton, I understand—"

"Please don't call me that," she interjected. "It implies a connection I do my utmost to forget. Besides, after what has just occurred, I believe we have crossed the boundaries of propriety."

Elliot snorted. "I think we crossed them way before that. But let me reiterate. If you wish to leave, I will find someone else to help you in your quest to find your sister."

"I don't want to leave." She paused and glanced down at her hands clasped together in front of her. "I … I have never known anyone I can talk to so easily. So, you have a terrible condition that is rather debilitating. I've known perfectly healthy men who are rotten to their core. What sort of person would I be to ask for your friendship only to stumble and reject you at the first hurdle?"

Grace Denton was the most remarkable woman he had ever met.

"You don't need to fear me, Grace."

"I know," she said with a smile. "Forgive me for storming in here and almost killing you. You have been far too kind to me and do not deserve to suffer for it."

Every minute he spent in her company caused a torturous agony to writhe in his chest and his belly.

"I presume whatever you wanted was urgent and could not wait."

She moved to the end of the bed, took the blanket and shook it out before draping it over his legs. Then she picked up her sister's diary from the floor. "It can wait until later. I'll give you some privacy so you can rest for a while. When you feel able, we'll talk then."

He couldn't help but smile. "I'll be up in a few hours." He was so tempted to ask her to stay, but he did not have the strength to fight his attraction to her. She didn't need to be seduced and pleasured by a scoundrel. The lady needed to be loved and cherished by a good man—things far beyond his meagre capabilities.

CHAPTER 6

"You're sure your brother and his wife are happy for me to stay with them for a few days?" The last thing Grace wanted was to be a nuisance. Not after all the trouble she'd caused this morning. "I thought they'd recently married. Won't it be somewhat awkward?"

The carriage turned sharply, forcing her to grab on to the seat for fear of tumbling forward into Lord Markham's lap. Whenever he looked at her, she recalled the pained expression in his eyes. She recalled the look of sheer terror when she'd yanked at the drapes. She had been equally scared—of him, of the strange, macabre change in his features, of the thought he might die. If only he'd told her of his terrible plight. But then she'd only known him for a day.

The realisation shocked her.

One day felt like one year.

The days spent in the company of Henry Denton ran into the hundreds, too many to count. Despite them all, he had been a relative stranger. Those ice-blue eyes would haunt her for a lifetime. The memory of such a lonely existence was more akin to gruelling torture.

She shivered at the thought.

The hours waiting for Lord Markham to rise had been spent in soulful contemplation. Whilst strolling in his garden, she'd considered a life trapped in the darkness. To never feel the sun's rays warm your skin, to never lose oneself in a blue sky, was a difficult thing to comprehend.

Like a slave to the night, he was chained to the darkness. Such restrictions must inevitably cause anger and frustration to simmer. Yet tonight he appeared composed, serene, unruffled.

"They're more than happy to have you to stay," he said, and she stared at his straight teeth as he talked, wondering what trick caused them to extend.

"It will only be for a few days." Without news of Caroline, she'd have no choice but to return to Cobham. She had no idea what to do next. Perhaps she should attend another event, pose as Caroline in the hope of gathering more information. She would have to go alone. It would be unfair to expect Lord Markham's assistance after everything he'd already done for her.

For the first time in three days, she pushed her feelings for Caroline aside.

These few private minutes were probably the last she would spend with Lord Markham. The thought caused a new wave of sadness. Regardless of his reputation, she liked him. She did not want the terrifying events of the day to taint her memory of him. Judging by his reaction to Caroline's criticism in her diary, she assumed he received little praise for his character. Well, she could do something about that.

"Before we reach your brother's house, I would like to say something." She swallowed deeply as her cheeks grew warm.

"Say what you will. But you do not need to apologise again for opening the drapes."

"I am truly sorry about that, but no. I want to tell you that … that you are perhaps the kindest, most honest gentleman I know. I do not care what others say or what they write about you in their silly little books. There are no words to express the depth of my gratitude for all you have done to help me."

Her throat felt so tight she dared not say another word.

Lord Markham's emerald eyes twinkled as his gaze drifted over her. She felt so hot she feared she'd set the seat ablaze.

One corner of his mouth curved up into a sinful smile. "You would not be so free with your compliments if you knew what I was thinking."

All the air left her lungs.

"Perhaps *thinking* is the wrong word," he continued in a playful tone. "*Imagining* seems much more appropriate."

He was teasing her, probably because he did not know how to take a compliment. "I did not say I didn't believe the salacious things I've heard. Just that I have been fortunate enough to meet the man, not the scoundrel."

"Don't dismiss the scoundrel." He raised an arrogant brow. "Granted, he has an entirely different range of talents. But you may find you like him all the more."

"I doubt it. A man who loves with his anatomy, as opposed to his heart, can never truly satisfy either himself or the woman he chooses to please."

Lord Markham snorted. "Would you care to put such an absurd theory to the test?"

The offer sounded surprisingly tempting. As a widow, she was free to pursue a liaison as long as she kept it discreet. But Grace smiled and shook her head.

"If your intention is seduction, you must do so with your character, my lord. I find boasting fills me with loathing, and the lack of genuine sentiment leaves me cold to my bones."

The thought of intimate relations purely to ease a physical urge brought memories of Henry flooding back. To lie with a man knowing he dreamed of another destroyed the soul. Recovery was slow and painful, and she would rather not experience it again.

Lord Markham leant forward and said softly, "If your intention is to seduce me with words, you're doing a remarkable job."

Grace folded her arms across her chest. "May I remind you, such flattery is conducive to failure."

"What if I told you I find you enchanting?" His voice sounded smooth and rich. "What if I said I had imagined raining kisses along the soft skin above your collarbone? That the sensations made you tremble while lying naked in my arms?"

Oh, he was extremely good at this game.

"Then I would tell you that your words are capable of rousing my desire. But such words cannot inflame my heart. Such words cannot stir a passion so deep I would die without it. I could never settle for anything less."

"Then you suggest I am doomed to fail. You should know, *failure* is not a word I am comfortable with."

She wondered if his illness made him bolder. If fighting against such rigid constraints is what forced him to avoid life's complications. One mistake and he could die. To live knowing your life dangled precariously surely hardened a heart to all emotion.

"You forget, I have experience of your heartless kisses. The memory is not one I care to revisit."

He sighed. "I agree. It was a pretty poor show. I won't make the same mistake again."

Grace's heart fluttered at the declaration. "It is the mark of a true gentleman to own up to one's faults."

"You value honesty, and so I am more than happy to give it to you."

Why did he make his last remark sound the most salacious of all?

The carriage ground to a halt, and she fell forward. Lord Markham put his hand on her elbow to steady her, the considerate gesture doing far more to warm her heart than his bawdy banter.

"I shall have a word with my coachman concerning his sloppy driving. I fear Gibbs can be quite reckless in his pursuits."

She smiled. "Well, they say the staff take their lead from their master."

He laughed, his eyes alight with amusement. "I concede," he said, holding up his hands after helping her down to the pavement. "You are the victor in this bout of quips. But know that I shall look forward to a rematch."

Lord Markham was still smiling when the butler escorted them into the hall and tapped lightly on a door to his left.

"Just give us a minute," a masculine voice boomed from behind the door.

Grace heard mumbling, giggling, what sounded like someone banging into a table.

Lord Markham coughed into his fist. "I think we have arrived at a rather inopportune moment."

"I told you this wasn't a good idea," Grace whispered.

"You may come in, Radley." A feminine voice called out to the butler. As he opened the door, they heard her whisper, "Will you stop it? Someone's here."

The butler, maintaining an impassive expression, announced them at once.

Lord Markham placed his hand at the small of her back and ushered her forward. "Mrs. Denton, may I present Lord and Lady Hale."

Offering a demure curtsy, Grace was surprised when Lady Hale stepped forward and took her hands. The lady had a rosy glow to her cheeks and strands of hair had fallen loose from her simple coiffure. "You must call me Evelyn," she said with a warm smile. "And my husband is Alexander. Any friend of Elliot's is a friend of ours."

Lady Hale walked over to Lord Markham. "Aren't you full of surprises?" she said as he brought her hand to his lips.

He offered an affectionate smirk. "It wouldn't do to be too predictable."

"Your brother tells me you're recently married," Grace said as Lady Hale gestured for her to sit down. Lord Markham sat beside her on the sofa, stretching his legs out languidly. "May I express my felicitations?"

Lord Hale narrowed his gaze. "You understand that we are not brothers in the usual sense?"

Lord Markham turned to her. "We are closer than family, hence my use of the term."

"Ignore Alexander," Lady Hale said. "They're brothers when it comes to the things that matter … friendship, trust and loyalty."

"Forgive me for disturbing you," Grace said. "I don't know what Lord Markham has told you regarding my circumstances."

"We understand your sister is missing," Lady Hale replied, her tone empathetic. "We understand you're on your own here in London, and Elliot feels it would be more appropriate if you did not stay at the home of an unmarried gentleman."

While Lady Hale did most of the talking, both Lord Hale and Lord Markham exchanged numerous glances, leading Grace to believe they were having a silent conversation.

"Not to mention the fact I almost killed him this morning," Grace added. "I'm sure he'll rest easier knowing I'm not about to tear into his chamber and rip open the drapes."

Lord Hale shot to his feet, his frantic gaze travelling over the length and breadth of Lord Markham. "Were you hurt?"

Lord Markham waved for him to sit. "A little scorched. Mrs. Denton mistook my reluctance to get up for indifference to her plight."

Yes, and for one heart-stopping moment, she had almost fainted at the shocking sight. "Thankfully, he had a decanter of bl— He had a drink to hand else I don't know what would have happened."

Both Lord and Lady Hale's mouths fell open, their eyes wide as they gaped at her.

Lord Hale cleared his throat. "Elliot told you about his affliction?"

"Of course. I have never been so frightened. His eyes were so terribly dark, almost black. I thought he was going to die."

Unless she was mistaken, Grace noticed Lady Hale smile. "Forgive me," Lady Hale began. "I do not mean to make light of such an awful experience. Elliot is such a private person. I … we are just surprised he told you."

"Under other circumstances, I doubt he would have mentioned it." Grace screwed up her nose and shook her head. "It is such a debilitating illness. I don't know how he manages."

"I am still here," Lord Markham said. "And I manage perfectly well. You make me sound like half a man."

Grace couldn't help but offer him a sultry smile. "I'm sure you do nothing in half measures, my lord."

His intense gaze drifted over her face before lingering on her lips.

Now it was Lord Hale's turn to smile. "You know, I do recall having a premonition in this room, not too long ago. When we were discussing who would be next to fall. You rebuked the notion that love—"

"Yes, yes. There's no need to drag it up," Lord Markham interjected. "I recall the conversation and am still of the same mind. As I explained to Mrs. Denton, I am not comfortable with intimacy."

"Indeed," Lord Hale replied as he studied her. "So you have led me to believe."

Lady Hale stood. "I assume you've not eaten, Mrs. Denton. I know how lax Elliot is when it comes to entertaining guests. Let me show you to your room while Mrs. Anderson prepares dinner."

Grace felt a little overwhelmed by their generous hospitality. She turned to Lord Markham, her heart lurching as she didn't know when she would see him again. "Will you be here when I return?"

Before he could answer, Lady Hale blurted, "Of course he'll

be here. Won't you, Elliot? He has no reason to rush home. Besides, Alexander wants him to stay."

Lord Hale looked up at his wife. "I do?" When she widened her eyes and nodded vigorously, he added. "Yes, I do. I'll get us a drink, Elliot. I think we both need one."

Lady Hale walked over and kissed her husband on the cheek. With a warm smile, he took her hand, caressed her palm with his thumb. "We won't be long. Elliot will keep you company."

As a couple, Lord and Lady Hale were openly affectionate. Even if they had never spoken a word, their love lit up the room. It was a stark contrast to the way she had felt with Henry and she struggled to suppress the melancholic mood taking hold.

Grace followed the lady up the stairs and to a door on the right. "I thought you might like this room. I've always found that yellow lifts the spirits."

From the pale lemon hangings to the deep gold walls, the room radiated a cheerful warmth that Grace found welcoming. "It's a beautiful room. I am so grateful to you for letting me stay."

Lady Hale sat down on the bed and patted the coverlet next to her. "Please, sit and tell me all about your sister."

Grace repeated everything she had told Lord Markham. After numerous attempts trying to call her Lady Hale, Grace finally conceded and agreed to call her Evelyn. Instinct told her she could trust Evelyn, and there was no point trying to present Caroline in a more favourable light.

"I understand your concern, Grace. I'm sure your sister would not have intentionally left you alone in the city. Elliot is an honourable man and will help you in any way he can."

"No doubt he feels obliged to help. I never really gave him much choice in the matter."

"Elliot is not a man who bows to obligation. Whatever he has done, he has done because he wants to." Evelyn placed her hand on Grace's arm. "His illness has hardened his heart. But underneath he is a good man."

"I must confess when I pulled back the drapes … when I first saw his face …" Grace swallowed as she recalled the shocking vision. "Had it not been for the fact he desperately needed me, I think I would have run away."

Evelyn sighed. "But thankfully you didn't. Elliot has been kind enough to help you. In return, you will help him."

"Help him?" She had no idea how to treat such an affliction. "I don't understand. I am not a doctor and know nothing of medicine."

Evelyn smiled. "I am not referring to his illness. Elliot believes he is incapable of caring for others, which is not the case at all. He needs a friend who can accept him for what he is, who will not judge him based on his strange affliction."

Grace recalled the lord's amorous words. "I think his idea of friendship is vastly different to mine."

Evelyn offered her a knowing smile.

"It's just that he knows of no other way to express himself. He hides in the dark. To him, it represents the absence of light, the loss of all that is good in him. Be his friend, Grace. He will fight it but show him it is what's in the heart that matters."

Grace did feel a burning need to offer the lord some comfort. But it would be on her terms. "Finding Caroline must be my priority. If Lord Markham continues to assist me, then I will consider all you have said."

"Excellent." Evelyn beamed. "Let us return to the gentlemen. We will break with convention and tell Mrs. Anderson we'll eat in the parlour."

As they walked back into the parlour, Grace's gaze flew to the empty sofa.

Evelyn looked about the room as Lord Hale stood. "Are you alone?" she asked with a hint of surprise.

Lord Hale cleared his throat. "Elliot offered his apologies. He has a prior engagement and has taken his leave. He asked me to tell you, Mrs. Denton, that he will make some enquiries whilst out, in the hope of finding your sister."

"What could be more important than his engagement here?" Evelyn sounded most put out.

"Erm … Lady Fortescue's ball. I believe he agreed to accompany Leo."

Grace suppressed her disappointment. She was familiar with the distraction techniques of men. Avoidance was by far the simplest way of dealing with any emotion.

Grace turned to Evelyn. "Would you mind if I went upstairs for a while?"

"Of course not. Would you like Mrs. Anderson to bring your dinner up to you?"

Grace forced a smile. "If it's no trouble."

"It's no trouble at all. And if you need anything more don't hesitate to ask."

As she climbed the stairs to her room, her thoughts drifted to her rogue of a dead husband. No one had spoken up for her. No one had come to her aid. She had been pushed and cajoled into a situation that had brought nothing but heartache.

Caroline had acted selfishly. Grace refused to let bitterness cloud her judgement and behave the same way.

Henry had acted abominably. Never again would she be ignored by a man or be treated as a worthless object, someone unworthy, inferior.

If Elliot Markham expected her to sit at home with her embroidery frame and wait for news, then he was sorely mistaken.

CHAPTER 7

"I want to hear it all," Leo said as they stared nonchalantly at the hordes of happy couples dancing. "Caroline Rosemond. Who would have thought?" He gave a drawn-out whistle. "And you said nothing could tempt you to accept an offer from such a celebrated courtesan."

"Nothing did," Elliot remarked cryptically, offering Lady Fortescue a respectful nod as she sauntered past.

For some unfathomable reason, he was tired of their usual antics. Looking for the next conquest had lost its appeal. Leo pointed out a few ladies alerting them to their availability by tapping their fans to their hearts. The irony of the gesture was not lost on him and brought to mind Grace Denton's insistence that lust without sentiment left her cold.

"You should avoid the ones with wigs and powdered faces," Elliot said with some amusement, "as you're sure to find nothing but frogs and toads beneath."

Leo raised a curious brow. "You're in a strange mood this evening." When Elliot didn't bother to reply, he added, "Well? Are you going to tell me why you took Miss Rosemond into your home? Why you have broken two of the rules you so rigidly observe?"

"I did not break them both," Elliot said with a sigh. "The lady you saw was not Caroline Rosemond." He did not give Leo a chance to show his surprise. "You're not to say a word to anyone. As a brother, I am asking for your discretion in the matter."

"Of course, although I fear you are in dire need of spectacles."

Just as there were similarities between the sisters, the differences were just as striking. As her name suggested, Grace possessed a natural elegance. Everything about Caroline was contrived. Grace's inner beauty shone through, whereas Caroline radiated nothing but conceit.

"The lady you met was Mrs. Denton, Caroline's sister. Miss Rosemond has not been seen for a few days. There's a fear something untoward has occurred."

As expected, Leo made an odd puffing noise. "She's probably off on some jaunt with her latest beau, lounging naked in front of a warm fire whilst being fed exotic fruit. Or perhaps she's in Brighton, frolicking in a bathing machine. But what has it all got to do with you?"

Leo's attention drifted to the luscious lady with honey-gold hair who walked past and brushed seductively against him. The obvious advance would usually rouse Elliot's amusement, and he'd make a merry quip in response. Yet tonight he could not shake the feeling of disdain.

He had left Alexander's house in haste. The need to spend a few uncomplicated hours, where he could ignore the range of newly awakened emotions flooding his mind and body, had proved futile. Talking about Grace Denton caused memories of their stimulating conversation in the carriage to resurface. In comparison, everything else felt so miserably dull and predictable.

"Caroline Rosemond wrote something about me in her diary," Elliot replied, tapping Leo on the arm to refocus his friend's attention. "She'd mentioned meeting a Markham, although Grace believes it may be short for something else."

"Grace?"

"I mean Mrs. Denton."

"I assume if she stayed the night with you then there is no Mr. Denton."

"She's a widow."

Leo placed his hand on Elliot's shoulder. "And so now you've sampled her wares you're out on the hunt once more."

Anger ignited. The sudden burst of fury forced him to knock Leo's hand away. "Do not speak of her in such base terms. It is nothing like that. She's a friend who needs my help."

Leo took an unsteady step back. His bottom lip practically hit the floor.

"Close your mouth," Elliot continued in a calmer tone. "Else you'll be gagging on powder and perfume for a month."

"I'm just surprised that's all. I've never known you speak so highly of any woman. Let alone one you've only known for a day."

Was it really only a day?

If he were openly courting her, the quality of time they'd spent together in the last twenty-four hours would equate to months. He did feel a strange connection to her. Perhaps because she wasn't fawning over him. Perhaps because she had rejected his advances.

His mind drifted then.

What would it take for her to succumb to his charms?

If only he could break through her rigid defences. Mr. Denton's skill in the bedchamber must have been terribly poor indeed. Else why would she believe that pleasure had more to do with emotion as opposed to how one used the relevant parts of their anatomy? It wouldn't take much to prove her wrong. Elliot knew a trick to curl her toes and have her begging for release.

Damn it. The thought caused his cock to pulse and throb.

Perhaps if he satisfied his needs with one of the ladies currently flashing him a generous eyeful of their bosom, he might banish all lustful dreams of Grace Denton. Clutching to the merits of that idea, he scanned the room.

No one roused his interest.

"I assumed Alexander would want to spend the night alone with his bride," Leo continued. "I know how he detests being out in Society."

Elliot shook his head and tried to focus on the conversation. "I did not bother to ask if he wished to attend. Besides, a ballroom is the last place he would choose to be, particularly when he is so besotted with Evelyn." He decided not to mention the fact they were entertaining a guest. "He's probably cuddled up on the chaise, reciting poetry and exchanging endearments, amongst other things."

A sharp pang of guilt hit him in the chest for leaving Grace Denton alone with the amorous couple.

"No, he's not," Leo said with a chuckle. "He's over there."

Leo pointed to the opposite side of the ballroom. Elliot raised his chin and narrowed his gaze to gain an optimum view.

"Don't be ridiculous. That can't be him," Elliot said, convinced there must be some mistake. Yes, the gentleman had broad shoulders and dark hair, but he suspected they would both chuckle with amusement when he turned around to reveal he was older or wore spectacles or had some absurd feature that set him apart.

"I swear that is Alexander. I saw him walk in."

The gentleman in question turned and scoured the room, his hard stare locking with Elliot's curious gaze. It took a moment for Elliot's brain to process the familiar vision before him.

Shock quickly replaced denial and then a deep sense of foreboding took hold. Without saying a word to Leo, Elliot pushed through the crowd, eager to discover the reason for Alexander's attendance.

On witnessing his approach, Alexander took a few steps towards him.

"You never mentioned you'd be here this evening," Elliot said, even more surprised to discover Evelyn standing at his side. He glanced over her shoulder, relieved to find they were alone. "I assume Mrs. Denton has settled in?"

Having the advantage of being a few inches taller, Alexander glared down at him. "Do not speak to me of Mrs. Denton," he said, through clenched teeth. "That woman has ruined my entire evening."

Evelyn threaded her arm through her husband's and hugged it. "Oh, don't say that. It wouldn't do if all nights were the same."

Alexander snorted. "It would do perfectly well for me."

"When will we next have an opportunity to waltz or listen to such a marvellous orchestra? And there may be no orangery here, but I hear Lady Fortescue has a wonderful hothouse."

Elliot grinned. "There are few gentlemen happy to admit to their love of flowers."

"You're not remotely funny," Alexander replied. "Next time you leave us to tend to one of your flock, at least have the decency to inform us we're harbouring a cunning wolf in the guise of a sweet little lamb."

"Well, I like her," Evelyn interjected. "I admire her tenacity and think she's incredibly brave."

Alexander gave a frustrated tut. "You mean you enjoyed playing dress maid."

"Well, you must admit, she looks angelic in white silk. Every gentleman in here has noticed."

"Yes, probably because they're not used to seeing a courtesan wear white."

Elliot was struggling to follow the conversation. "I'm afraid you lost me with the wolf and lamb analogy."

Evelyn put her hands on her hips. "Grace is not a courtesan."

Elliot turned to Alexander. "What has Mrs. Denton done to

deserve your wrath?" He imagined she'd have been nothing but charming, wishing nothing more than to express her thanks and gratitude for their generous hospitality.

"Is it not obvious?" Alexander opened his arms wide. "Why else would I be trussed up like a partridge? It is your fault for running off and leaving her alone."

Elliot followed Alexander's disapproving glare and Evelyn's look of affection and pride to the figure of Grace Denton, busily engaged in dancing the cotillion with Lord Dunn.

"What the blazes?" Elliot whispered through gritted teeth as his heart hit his ribs with all the force of cannon fire.

"Doesn't she look beautiful?" Evelyn mused. "Katie worked wonders with her hair."

With a brilliant smile and a burst of lively enthusiasm, Grace Denton and her partner followed the head couple through the set of elaborate steps. The first sparks of jealousy ignited, simmering beneath Elliot's composed facade and he swallowed to shift the lump in his throat.

"Have you lost your mind?" Elliot focused his pent up frustration on Alexander. "She cannot be seen out in Society. And assuming people believe she's a courtesan she is hardly suitable company for your wife."

"Don't you think I know that?" Alexander spat. "I had to escort Evelyn inside and then go back and have a quiet word with Lady Fortescue. A little gentle persuasion and it appeared Caroline Rosemond had been invited after all. Lord Dunn was more than pleased to play escort, hence the reason they are currently hopping about together."

"What does she hope to gain by attending?" Elliot threw his hands in the air, feeling the need to do something other than stand there gaping.

"Oh, trust me. She has thought it through." Alexander's words brimmed with sarcasm. "It appears the lady has composed a list of all potential villains and is keen to get to work on solving the mystery of her missing sister."

Evelyn leant forward and whispered, "We found her sneaking out of the house. Her intention was to return home to Arlington Street to change before making her way here."

Offering an incredulous glare, Elliot asked, "Does she expect one of the suspects to hold up their hands and admit to any wrongdoing?"

"Well, we've had a little breakthrough with the diary." Evelyn actually sounded excited. "And before we—"

"There's no *we* about it," Alexander said. "You're not helping her, Eve."

Evelyn shot him a determined look. "And what if Elliot had refused his assistance? Without the use of his carriage, you would have never reached me in time. Heaven knows what would have happened to me. And what if he had not found me in the forest—" She stopped abruptly and sucked in a deep breath.

Alexander took her gloved hand and brought it to his lips. "I do not care to be reminded." He turned to Elliot. "We will, of course, help in any way we can."

Elliot glanced back at the dancers, noting the more dissolute gentlemen hovering around the floor eager for a bit of sport. "I need to get her out of here. From a distance people will assume she's Caroline. But once they speak to her, it's obvious she's not."

"Her intention this evening is to speak with Mr. Hamilton," Evelyn informed him. "She wonders if the Markham is short for Marcus Hamilton."

Marcus Hamilton was a renowned rogue, but gambling was his love and Elliot could not imagine him wasting his time or effort on spiriting away a courtesan.

"Her sister mentioned the gentleman a few times in her diary," Evelyn continued. "Once Grace is convinced he played no part in her sister's disappearance we will move more towards my theory."

"Your theory?" Elliot asked, trying to focus on the conversation. The dancers were leaving the floor, and he needed to keep watch of his quarry.

"That Caroline often used a few words to represent a time, person and place."

Elliot noticed Lord Dunn escort Grace over to converse with Marcus Hamilton and the muscles in his abdomen hardened in response.

"She is not safe here," he suddenly blurted.

Guilt delivered another stab to his chest. He should have stayed with her. He should have known she would not snuggle up under the coverlet and leave it all to him, although solving the mystery of Miss Rosemond's disappearance was not really on his agenda. In truth, Grace Denton was better off without her.

"Then you will need to persuade her to leave." Alexander took his wife's hand and placed it in the crook of his arm. "I assume you've brought your carriage?" When Elliot nodded, he said. "Good. I will take Evelyn outside for a stroll in the garden while you talk to Mrs. Denton. Let's agree to meet at the end of the street in thirty minutes."

"Agreed," Elliot said. He gave a loud sigh. "Well, I suppose I had better round up the wolf."

Alexander smiled. "I have a feeling she might growl a little and flash her teeth."

"But mine are sharper," he whispered, "and far more lethal."

"Just have a care. You have already beaten one gentleman to protect her honour. Let us hope the lady doesn't drive you to massacre a whole ballroom."

Elliot offered a weak smile. The way he felt at the moment, anything was possible.

After watching his friends make their way to the terrace, Elliot turned his attention to Grace Denton. Marcus Hamilton laughed at something she said. He knew only too well the look of a man intent on seduction. When the devil's gaze dropped to her spectacular breasts, the burning sensation in Elliot's chest was akin to swallowing a scalding-hot beverage. He exhaled deeply to rein in his ire.

When the gentleman touched her arm, Grace almost stumbled in her haste to step back. Jealousy flared, coupled with an overwhelming need to protect her. Elliot clenched his jaw to prevent his teeth from extending as he strode towards them, feeling a sudden urgency to intervene.

CHAPTER 8

"I still can't quite put my finger on it," Mr. Hamilton said, tapping the aforementioned finger to his lips as his gaze lingered on her mole. His voice held a rich, seductive quality as though his words were not in accordance with the lascivious nature of his thoughts. "Is it the way you've styled your hair, I wonder? Or is it the air of innocence you're trying so hard to convey? There is definitely something different about you."

Thank goodness the gentleman had consumed a fair few drinks.

"You do not appear shocked to see me," Grace said, trying her best to use her sister's flirtatious tone. But she lacked the teasing sway of the shoulders and the alluring pout that came naturally to Caroline.

"I'm shocked you approached me that is all. I thought we were done with." He continued to peruse her from head to toe, his eyes gleaming as though they had the power to see through numerous layers of clothing. "But alas, you know I cannot fund the lifestyle you require. Not when I would rather spend my funds at the tables."

"And so you choose gambling over love, sir."

Her response seemed to puzzle him, and he narrowed his gaze.

With a gloved hand, he touched the tips of his fingers to her upper arm and despite her shuffling back he did not break contact. "I think we both know love played no part in our … vigorous activities. I'm not saying no. I'm just saying I can't pay."

Bile bubbled away in her stomach as she struggled to hide a look of contempt. What on earth had Caroline seen in this wretch of a man? She wanted to tell him she would sooner lie down with a leper. But to do so would be to imply money was the overriding factor in all of Caroline's liaisons and she could not bring herself to admit to something so dreadful.

"You will have to give me time to consider all you've said." Nerves pushed to the fore as she tried to extricate herself from this awkward situation, which was all of her own making.

"What is there to think about?"

Grace took a step back, causing his fingers to fall from her arm. "I … I made a mistake. I thought … I thought …"

"You thought what?" he said arrogantly. "You thought that I would fall at your feet like the rest of them? I told you. You're not worth a guinea."

Grace choked back a sob as she struggled to maintain her composure. In her head, she imagined punching him on the nose. She imagined him crumpling to the floor, his starched cravat dripping with blood.

When she opened her mouth to speak, nothing came out.

She felt a hand at the small of her back and turned to see Lord Markham's handsome face. Relief caused her shoulders to sag. As he studied her, she saw the muscle in his jaw twitch, saw anger flare in his vibrant green eyes, noticed the odd fleck of black.

"Miss Rosemond. I believe ours is the next dance."

Mr. Hamilton snorted. "Have you got a guinea to hand? I'm sure the lady has change."

The air about them whirled with a wild, volatile tension. She knew Lord Markham was ready to release the Devil's own fury.

"Don't," she whispered, placing her hand lightly on his arm. "It's not worth it. He's not worth it."

Lord Markham tore his gaze away from Mr. Hamilton.

"It will only draw undue attention," she added by way of an inducement.

Lord Markham nodded yet his expression remained dark.

"I thought you'd be at the card game, Hamilton," he said as he stared deeply into the rogue's eyes.

"Card game?"

"The one at the house in Bow Street. I hear Malesbury has a fortune to lose. I recall seeing your name on the list. Yes, I'm sure they're expecting you."

Hamilton's eyes glazed over, and Grace thought he might stumble. "Bow Street?" he mumbled. "They're expecting me?"

"They're expecting you now," Lord Markham reiterated, his gaze intense. "You must not forget to knock on the window with three loud raps and shout the password."

"Three raps and shout the password."

Lord Markham stepped closer and whispered, "The password is *down with the monarchy*. I would knock on every window, just to be certain." When Hamilton stared at him, Elliot repeated, "Go to Bow Street. Knock on every window. Shout *down with the monarchy*."

Mr. Hamilton nodded. "I … I had best be on my way."

Astounded, Grace watched the man scurry away. "He seems set on doing exactly what you told him. Is it a conjurer's trick?"

"The mind is weak in certain individuals," he replied. "And as such, can be easily manipulated if you know how."

Grace remembered feeling strange when she first met Lord Markham. "Did you try to use the same trick on me?"

"Trust me. There is nothing weak about your mind. The insane often have the strongest minds of all."

"Insane?" She batted him playfully on the arm. "At least Mr.

Hamilton thought he was talking to Caroline when he insulted me."

Lord Markham's eyes still burned with anger, and he glanced back over his shoulder. "Let us go somewhere more private and then I'll tell you why I'm so damnably annoyed."

Without saying another word, he placed her hand in the crook of his arm and escorted her from the ballroom. The muscles bulging against the sleeve of his coat felt taut and rigid, ready to burst through the material without warning. She could have argued with his high-handed approach. But it would only draw unnecessary attention.

He stopped at the end of a long corridor. The walls were covered with paintings of men in long white wigs all looking as equally stern, all ready to condemn the guilty to the gallows.

"What on earth were you thinking?" he said, backing her into an alcove. "After what happened with Barrington everyone will be talking about you. You cannot risk someone discovering your identity. I swear I almost ripped Hamilton's head from his shoulders for what he said to you. My heart is still racing. God help anyone else should make a derogatory comment as I don't think I can stop myself."

Grace couldn't help but smile. Yes, he was extremely angry. Yes, she had been out of her depth with the likes of Mr. Hamilton. And yes, she was in danger of finding herself in another threatening situation. But it was what Lord Markham hadn't said that caused the corners of her mouth to curl.

Grace put her hand to his cheek. "Thank you for caring."

He blinked, looked shocked, completely taken aback. His ragged breathing slowed to a calmer rate, and he closed his eyes and inhaled deeply.

Struggling with her own overwhelming feelings, she lowered her hand.

Lord Markham opened his eyes slowly, his heated gaze scorching her soul. "What are you doing to me?" he whispered.

Feeling a little bolder she said, "I am using a part of my

anatomy, coupled with honest sentiment, to incite a genuine reaction. What was it that touched you? Was it the feel of my hand or hearing the emotion behind the gesture?"

He swallowed visibly. "Both."

"Well, I think that proves my point, don't you? And I must say, I find you far more appealing when you speak from the heart."

A sinful smile touched his lips. "Perhaps I should try it more often."

Grace nodded. "I think you should."

They simply stared at each other for a moment and she suddenly wondered what it would feel like to be held in his arms, to feel his lips move over hers with genuine affection. Henry Denton had rarely kissed her. Even when inclined, it had amounted to nothing more than a peck on her cheek or the faintest touch to the top of her head.

Anger threatened to flare.

Why did everything always come back to her feelings about Henry?

Perhaps she would never recover from the hurt and betrayal. Was every thought and action to be overshadowed by past experiences?

"While your bawdy banter always leaves me cold," she said playfully, pushing all other feelings aside, "your honest reaction leaves me wondering if your skin tastes of sandalwood. If, despite your licentious nature, your lips are capable of moving softly and tenderly."

She could only surmise that her frustration with Henry had caused her to speak so boldly.

"Why spend your time wondering?" His wicked emerald gaze lingered on her lips. "Why not put me to the test? Use me to satisfy your curiosity."

Grace had expected the logical part of her brain to dismiss the idea as ludicrous, yet she found herself intrigued by Elliot Markham.

"I do not think it would do much for your reputation to be seen cavorting with Caroline Rosemond."

"I would not be cavorting with Caroline Rosemond. I would be cavorting with you, Grace. I would be kissing you, sweetly, gently, savouring every single second."

Excitement raced through her. A blazing fire settled hot and heavy between her thighs. The feeling was strange to her. She felt a little dizzy, as though she'd drunk too much punch at Christmas. And she was in danger of becoming lost in the moment.

"Not here," she said, and the words came out more like a gasp.

"Where then?" His chest rose and fell more rapidly as he moistened his lips.

For some obscure reason, she imagined her bed at home in Cobham. *Don't think about Henry*, she thought, repeating the words over and over in her mind. But he was there again, hot and sweaty, heaving above her as she lay like a cold slab of marble, wanting to cry.

"I can't." She bit down on her trembling lip, aware of his look of confusion.

There was something wrong with her.

She was not like other women.

When he shook his head, she expected him to shout, to berate her for her inadequacy. "We need to get you home," he said, his tone revealing his frustration. "Evelyn and Alexander will be expecting us. We can talk about Evelyn's theory regarding the notes in the diary and decide what we should do next."

Her heart blossomed at his reaction. He had not made her feel awkward or ashamed.

"I need to use the retiring room." It would give her a moment to compose herself.

"I'll wait for you here."

She gave him a weak smile and headed down the hall to the room reserved for ladies to attend to their needs.

The room appeared to be a less formal drawing room; the numerous dressing screens made it seem small and compact. The air was heavy with the sickly sweet smell of a variety of perfumes. She nodded to the two ladies standing in front of the large gilt mirror, only aware of their interest in her when she heard one of them call out her name.

"Miss Rosemond."

Grace groaned inwardly. She was tired of acting, tired of being anything other than herself. But she turned and smiled. "Good evening" was all she could think to say.

One lady stepped forward, her ebony ringlets framing a petite porcelain-white face. "May I offer my condolences on the terrible circumstance you recently found yourself in?" Her tone lacked the sincerity her words conveyed, and Grace grew suspicious of her motives. What terrible circumstance was she referring to?

"Thank you," Grace replied, sensing the woman's desperation to reveal all she knew.

"I'm afraid there were a few who witnessed Lord Barrington's poor pugilistic skills." The lady's dark brown eyes scanned her face, focused on the mole on her cheek as if it were a rare artefact in a museum. There was something distrusting about her countenance. Every look was more of an examination, an assessment.

"Hopefully, the gentleman understands I have no wish to entertain him further." Grace tried to be as vague as possible.

The lady smiled, but it did not reach her eyes. "Lord Barrington is an oaf." She leant forward and whispered, "But do tell all. I am curious to know of Lord Markham's involvement. Some say he is smitten with you."

"Lord Markham is not the sort of man to keep a lover, as I am sure you're aware." Grace refused to offer anything more. "And *smitten* is a word foreign to his vocabulary."

Grace had no idea how Caroline would react in conversation with women of such quality. Would a courtesan converse with well-bred ladies? In doing so, had she unwittingly revealed her secret?

"If you will excuse me," Grace said, and without further comment left the room.

"Are you ready?" Lord Markham took a few steps towards her.

"Just wait a moment. Pretend we are talking about something. I want you to watch the door and tell me who the lady is with the ebony ringlets."

"Why?" A frown marred his brow while his tone carried a hint of concern.

"Perhaps I'm paranoid. Perhaps the events of the last few days have addled my weary brain. But I believe there is a lady in the retiring room who knows I am not Caroline. I have a feeling she knew so before even speaking to me."

"Well, ladies are far more astute than gentlemen when it comes to noticing such things."

Grace heard the door open behind her and watched Lord Markham take a discreet peek over her shoulder.

"It's Lady Sudley," he continued. "I mean no disrespect when I say this, but a lady of her standing would usually snub the likes of Caroline Rosemond."

"I am not offended," she said with a sigh. "In the last few days, I seem to have grown accustomed to hearing slanderous remarks about my sister. Then again, I don't suppose they can be called slanderous when they're true."

Lord Markham offered an empathetic smile but did not contradict her. "There is a difference between suspecting you're not Caroline and knowing so. The latter implies some level of involvement."

"We will talk about Evelyn's theory and then decide what to do tomorrow." Tonight, she was done with thinking. She needed a clear head if she was to help Caroline.

Lord Markham removed his pocket watch and glanced at the time. “I said we would meet Alexander and Evelyn outside. We had better make our apologies and leave.”

Grace allowed him to escort her back to Evelyn’s house on Duke Street. In the small confines of his carriage, she was conscious of him sitting so close. In his presence, she felt safe, protected. Evelyn sat next to her husband, smiling as her gaze shifted between them.

But one terrifying thought overshadowed all others.

Her fears had nothing to do with Caroline or Lady Sudley or whatever devious schemes were at work. The closer she became to Lord Markham, the more she knew that Henry Denton’s presence still lingered within her. It tainted her blood, contaminated her memories, poisoned her future.

She had to find a way to be free of him.

She had to find a way to cleanse her soul.

CHAPTER 9

The constant rocking of the carriage on the uneven road did little to settle Elliot's chaotic mind.

He had tried to listen to Grace's thoughts; he had tried to determine what it was that troubled her so deeply. Henry Denton's name had drifted into his mind, accompanied by feelings of anguish, loneliness and pain. The sins of a selfish husband had left a permanent scar which he feared was still somewhat raw.

In his mind, he imagined putting a comforting arm around her shoulder, drawing her to his chest where it was warm, safe.

Elliot had never claimed to be an honourable man, not when it came to his sexual appetite. Indeed, half of him could think of nothing other than burying himself deep inside Grace Denton. To sate a physical need. To satisfy a curiosity.

Half of him wanted to offer his protection, to ease her fears, make her happy.

That's the part that terrified him, the part he struggled to understand.

Evelyn cleared her throat. "If you're not too tired, we could look through your sister's diary, and I could tell you more about my theory."

"No," Grace said with a sigh. "I'm not tired."

Elliot cast Grace a sideways glance and knew from her demeanour that she was simply being polite. The last few days must have taken their toll. Sometimes she appeared so confident, so controlled and determined. But the times when she appeared lost, a little fragile and broken seemed to manifest more frequently as the hours passed.

Of course, she only had a matter of days to uncover the mystery surrounding Caroline Rosemond's disappearance. He did not envy her the task of explaining her sister's demise to her mother.

And he had not helped matters. His negligence had forced her to put herself at risk tonight.

"I think we should focus all our efforts on helping Mrs. Denton discover what has happened to Miss Rosemond," he said with a level of determination he rarely expressed.

Alexander raised a brow. "Then we will need to be open and honest. We will need a structured plan, follow some logical order." He focused his attention on Grace. "Forgive me, but you cannot go barging into ballrooms in the hope someone will unwittingly reveal information."

"I'm sure she only did what she thought best," Elliot said, feeling the need to come to her defence. He could berate her for her folly, but he'd be damned if anyone else could.

"Lord Hale is right," Grace said, fiddling with her fingers in her lap. "I was angry and frustrated, although the evening was not a complete waste of time."

The carriage rumbled to a halt outside the house on Duke Street.

"Let's continue our conversation in the parlour," Evelyn added before turning to Grace. "Would you mind if we all examine the diary? I know you allowed me to flick through while Katie dressed your hair, but if you'd rather we—"

"No, it's fine. We need to work together. Finding Caroline is what's important."

There was the faintest trace of resentment in Grace's words, and Elliot wondered if she had spent her whole life pandering to her sister's whims and demands. If they discovered her sister had been gallivanting off on some wild jaunt, Elliot would string her up from a tree on the common and leave her as food for the crows.

As they made their way inside, he put his hand on Alexander's arm causing him to stop abruptly. "You've blood here I assume? I am in need of something soothing to drink."

He inclined his head. "Wait for us in the parlour, Evelyn. We will be but a few minutes."

They moved into the drawing room and Alexander rang the bell. "Is this just about blood?" he asked dubiously. "I have a suspicion it's about Mrs. Denton."

"I do need a drink. And I do need to ask you something. But first, let me apologise for leaving Grace alone here. I did not expect it to be such an inconvenience."

"It's not that I didn't want to help you. You must understand, my motives are purely selfish. I enjoy being alone with Evelyn and I get somewhat angry and frustrated when things don't go to plan."

There was a light rap on the door and Mrs. Shaw scuttled in. "Yes, my lord?"

"Could you bring us both some refreshment? We'll drink in here. Thank you, Mrs. Shaw."

"Right you are, my lord." The old woman gave a merry nod and waddled away.

"I understand," Elliot said. "I do not suppose this was how you envisaged spending the first week of married life."

"As always, Evelyn has the right of it. Without your help, we might never have married. So, I promise to stop sulking and to concentrate my efforts in helping Mrs. Denton. Besides, the sooner we solve the mystery, the sooner I can take Evelyn home to Hampshire."

Elliot chuckled. He was beginning to see the attraction of

devoting all one's time and effort to one woman, and as Mrs. Shaw returned with their drinks, he said, "How did you feel in the beginning? How did you feel when you first met Evelyn?"

Alexander gestured to the chair, and they both sat down and swallowed a mouthful of blood. "Confused. I concentrated all my efforts on being angry. It was a way of suppressing the need she roused in me. I struggled to fight the attraction. I think you know the rest."

"Was it a purely physical attraction?" Elliot asked. He feared his fascination with Grace went beyond sexual gratification. The thought of navigating uncharted waters unnerved him.

"Yes, but it was more than that," Alexander replied. "I feel different when I'm with her. It is as though we are the only two people in the world who speak the same language."

"Mrs. Denton believes that if a man is ever to satisfy a woman, he must love with his heart not just his anatomy." Elliot stared at Alexander as he almost spurted blood all over his evening clothes. "Do you think it's true?"

Recovering quickly, Alexander pondered the question. "If anyone were listening to this conversation, they would think we've lost our minds. But yes, I suppose it's true. Don't ask me to explain it. You must discover it for yourself." Alexander sighed and narrowed his gaze. "Elliot, in the short time I've known you, you have always struck me as a man in complete control, of your life, your wants and desires. If Grace Denton has caused some change in you, then you owe it to yourself to pursue the possibility that there could be more to it than a fanciful attraction." He snorted. "Now I sound like a matron offering advice to a debutante."

Elliot rubbed his chin as he contemplated his friend's words. "My idea of pursuing the possibility is to use more licentious means. I doubt there are many matrons willing to offer the same advice."

They sat in silence for a moment.

"What do you know of Mr. Denton?" Alexander enquired.

Elliot shrugged. "Not much. He's dead—"

"I know that."

"She was married to him for a few months, a loveless arrangement, I gather. I sense a deep passion within her. But it is anchored down by the weight of a heavy burden."

"Perhaps he was unkind to her. Cold, even."

"Perhaps." It appeared the disappearance of Caroline Rosemond was not the only mystery to solve. Somehow, he suspected the more he knew of Mr. Denton, the more he would understand Grace.

Was he bothered enough to pursue the matter?

Damn right he was.

He had made up his mind. Nothing would deter him from his course. He wanted Grace Denton and would do whatever was necessary to achieve his goal.

They returned to the parlour to find Evelyn and Grace huddled next to one another on the sofa. Evelyn had the diary in her lap and was using the tip of her finger as a guide as she scanned the page.

"Look, here's another one." Evelyn's eyes were alight with excitement. "This one says two … George … and it looks like Jerm."

Grace glanced over Evelyn's shoulder. "So you think she was to meet with George at two o'clock and at a place that sounds like Jerm?"

"Could be Jermyn Street," Elliot said, deciding to sit in the chair opposite and join the conversation.

"Why would she write it in code?" Alexander asked, standing in front of them with his hands clasped behind his back. "Why would she have to be so secretive if it's in her personal diary?"

Evelyn shook her head and tutted. "We are reading it.

Perhaps she feared someone else might discover it? I'm sure she must have had gentlemen call at her home. She probably thought it was more discreet to record it this way."

"Oh, she didn't worry about being discreet when slandering my character," Elliot scoffed.

Grace raised a brow in censure. "That's just gossip. There is a difference between recording one's own opinion and keeping a record of secret liaisons."

"Here's another one. Only this one is a meeting a few days before her disappearance." Evelyn narrowed her gaze and focused on the script. "It says twelve … Hodges … forty-two Pic."

Elliot could think of only two possible places. "Well, it's either Pickering Place—"

"There are only two reasons to go to Pickering Place," Alexander said, dropping into a chair. "To visit a gaming hell or to pay off a gaming debt."

"Or fight a duel," Elliot added, "although I've not heard of one fought there in years. The gentlemen tend to venture out of town."

Grace gasped. "You can't think Caroline was involved in either of those things."

Alexander raised a dubious brow. "Perhaps there was an argument over her affections. If we're going to investigate, we'll need to go tomorrow evening. But you should know I'm appallingly bad at cards."

Evelyn chuckled. "You're in such a rush to go to a gaming hell that you've missed a vital piece of information. What does the forty-two mean? If it is a door number then it begs the question, is there a forty-two Pickering Place?"

"There's a forty-two Piccadilly," Elliot said. "It's either the apothecary or the bookshop and stationers. It's a few doors away from one of the finest brandy merchants and is also opposite the church."

Alexander coughed into his fist. "I suspect it's a few years since you've squashed into a pew on a Sunday morning."

"More than a few I'd say. But I never shirk my responsibilities when it comes to brandy. I also used to frequent the apothecary. Now my footman has inherited the task. I like their sandalwood shaving soap."

Grace smiled. "Well, perhaps I can collect your order. I'm sure it won't hurt if I call by in the morning and browse their wares, see if the proprietor's name is Hodges."

"Oh, I could come with you," Evelyn said. "With your hair hidden in a bonnet, no one will pay you any heed."

While Alexander protested, Elliot watched Grace. She seemed more relaxed, happier even. He liked the way her pretty blue eyes sparkled when she spoke of more pleasant things. He wondered how they'd look if he lavished her with attention. He imagined his nimble fingers rousing a response, knew she would glow, exude radiance in the aftermath of her release.

The throbbing ache in his loins caused him to shift uncomfortably in the chair.

When he refocused his attention, he noticed Alexander was standing. "It is impossible for me to accompany you."

Evelyn patted Grace on the arm. "Alexander suffers from the same affliction as Elliot." When Alexander clenched his jaw and widened his eyes in alarm, she added, "We can trust Grace not to reveal your secret."

Grace appeared almost happy at the news. "On my life, I will not speak a word of it," she said, putting her hand to her chest. "In truth, it pleases me to know that Lord Markham is not suffering alone. I imagine it can be quite an isolating condition."

All heads turned to look at Elliot.

His chest felt warm. His cock pulsed with the need to reward Grace for her caring comment. "It can be lonely at times," he heard himself say. They were words he had never uttered before, not in company, not even to himself. But he recognised the truth in them, knew they formed the basis of all his hidden fears. The need to be intimate with her, to drive away the debilitating thoughts, pushed to the fore.

Alexander must have sensed his torment as he turned to Grace and changed the subject. “Earlier, in the carriage, you said the evening was not entirely wasted. What did you mean by it?” Alexander clasped his hands behind his back again as he waited for her reply.

Grace looked up at him. “A lady approached me in the retiring room.”

“It was Lady Sudley,” Elliot informed.

“She expressed concern over the incident with Lord Barrington and enquired as to Lord Markham’s involvement.” Grace glanced at Elliot, as she had not mentioned the lady had asked about him. “She studied my reaction with interest, studied my features. It seemed odd.”

“More than likely, she’s only interested in gossip.” Alexander waved his hand in the air dismissively. “It’s to be expected. But I’m certain they’ll be talking about someone else tomorrow.”

Something niggled away at the back of Elliot’s mind. “I’m just surprised a lady of her standing would converse with a courtesan.”

Alexander shrugged. “Perhaps being in the retiring room offered an opportunity too good to miss. To be the bearer of such a juicy piece of scandal would place her in an elevated position amongst her peers.”

Appearing oblivious to their conversation, Evelyn tore her gaze away from the diary. “So, the night Caroline disappeared, she met with someone called Mark at nine o’clock.” She turned to Grace. “Did she leave in the evening?”

Grace nodded. “And she walked so it couldn’t have been too far.”

Elliot sat forward. “Does she always walk the streets alone at night? Did you not caution her regarding such folly?”

Grace gave a resigned sigh. “No one can tell Caroline what

to do. She makes up her own mind and never yields even when she's wrong."

There it was again, Elliot thought, the slight hitch in her voice. He suspected she had borne the brunt of Caroline's selfishness on many occasions.

"The *ham* could stand for Ham Yard or Hampstead Street," Elliot said, clutching at anything that meant shifting the focus away from his name. "But both of those places are too far to walk to at night."

Evelyn closed the diary and handed it back to Grace. "I think we need to go back before we can move forward. We need to build a picture of where she went before she disappeared."

Alexander folded his arms across his chest. "You mean you want to go shopping in Piccadilly."

"Snooping not shopping," Evelyn said with a grin. "And in the evening, you may go to a gaming hell."

"I am not half as excited as you are." Alexander grimaced.

Evelyn turned to Grace and patted her arm. "We'll leave mid-morning."

Grace offered a grateful smile and turned to Elliot. "Could I trouble you for one more thing this evening?"

She could ask him for anything, and he would gladly oblige. His wicked mind conjured all sorts of salacious scenarios. The hard lump in his throat felt like nothing compared to the hard lump in his breeches.

"Of course," he said, bowing his head.

"You have your carriage here. Would you mind escorting me to Arlington Street?"

Elliot's heart skipped a beat as he narrowed his gaze. "Not with the intention of remaining there?"

"No." She shook her head. "I think it prudent to be certain Caroline has not returned before we go racing around town on a fool's errand."

It was a logical request.

"If we find her lounging on the chaise, I swear I will not be able to curb my tongue or my temper."

Grace snorted. "If we find her lounging on the chaise, I'll be the first to hit her over the head with a chamber pot."

In truth, he did not feel anger towards Caroline Rosemond. Not for leaving her sister alone without saying a word, not even for writing his name in her blasted diary.

How could he?

If anything, he owed her a debt of gratitude for the beautiful gift she had left behind. For the only woman who had ever penetrated his arrogant facade. The only woman capable of warming his cold heart.

CHAPTER 10

As soon as they stopped outside her sister's house in Arlington Street, Grace knew they would not find Caroline inside. The house was too dark, looked desolate and lonely.

"I shall enter first." Elliot stepped in front of her like an errant knight ready to protect her with his shield. She clutched his sleeve as they navigated the gloomy hallway. The cold air held a damp, earthy smell, supporting her theory that the house still lay empty.

"Thank you for agreeing to come with me," she whispered.

Having spent two days alone in the house, she should have had no problem nipping back in on her own. But Elliot would not hear of it. How very different he was from Henry.

After checking the rooms leading off the hallway, Grace tapped Elliot's arm. "Perhaps we should check her bedchamber."

"What about the kitchen?"

"I doubt Caroline would even know where it is," she said with a chuckle.

"While we're here, we may as well conduct a thorough search."

"Very well."

They made their way to the kitchen. Despite growing accustomed to the darkness, it took a few seconds to identify the black shadow sitting on the old table. The wicker basket contained provisions: bread, eggs, a jar of preserves amongst other things.

"This wasn't here before." Her voice revealed her surprise as she examined the contents.

Elliot picked up the cube of wrapped butter, turned it over in his hand and then placed it back into the basket. "One of her servants must have brought it here for you. But why leave? Why not stay?"

"Perhaps she did wait but thought I'd gone back to Cobham." Grace stamped the floor in frustration. "It was wrong of me to leave. I should have stayed. I should have waited. Mrs. Jones might have been able to tell me more."

"There's no point dwelling on it now. Besides, Barrington is far too unstable. You would not wish to be here alone if he came knocking."

Grace snorted. "Instability is a trait I am used to dealing with."

She met his intense gaze. His emerald eyes sparkled sinfully in the dark. It felt as though her stomach held a thousand loose feathers, all floating about in a bid to torment and tickle.

"Are you referring to your husband or your sister?" he asked.

"Both," she said with a weary sigh.

There was a brief silence before he asked, "Did he hurt you?"

"Who? Henry?" An odd chuckle escaped from her lips, the sound far from revealing any hint of happiness. "He hurt me in many ways. Too many to mention."

Too many to forget, she added silently.

Grace looked to the floor and focused on erasing the stains that were her memories. She knew how to suppress them. But the sullied marks always remained. Lord Markham stepped around the table and placed his hands on her upper arms.

"If your husband were alive, I would bloody well kill him."

There was a truth to his words that touched her soul. If only she had known him before. If only he could have been her champion. It pleased her that he could curse in her company. Lord Markham never treated her like a child. He never disrespected her.

"Why are you helping me?" The words tumbled out of her mouth without thought.

His gaze drifted over her face, falling to her lips, and he sucked in a breath. "Why have you allowed me to?"

"Give me an honest answer, and I promise to reciprocate."

Beneath his soothing touch her arms felt warm, the heat spreading rapidly through her body. With him standing so close, she struggled to focus. And the pulsing sensation beat its seductive rhythm at the apex of her thighs.

He smiled. "Perhaps I enjoy playing knight-errant to a damsel in distress."

"Is that all?" The hint of disappointment in her tone was unmistakable. "Is that the only reason?"

"I like you, Grace. More than you want me to. More than I care to admit."

"How do you know what I want?"

He shrugged. "I know you don't want me to kiss you."

Oh, he was wrong.

She'd thought of nothing else all day, dreamt of nothing else all night. Amidst the noise and bustle of the ballroom, she had wanted desperately to be held in his arms. Would it feel as comforting as she imagined? But fear, like a devil on her shoulder, whispered its evil words. What if he became too rough? What if she wanted him to stop, and he refused to listen?

Henry's twisted grin flashed into her mind. Were those cold eyes and callous lips to haunt her forever?

"Kiss me if you wish to," she suddenly said, hoping the touch of an angel would banish the Devil.

He removed his hat, placed it on the table and brushed his hands through his ebony locks. "Do you want me to kiss you, Grace?"

"Yes." Each breath came more quickly as he scanned her face, moistened his lips. "Be gentle with me," she said. "Don't rush me."

He brushed her hair from her cheek, cupped her face in his hands. "I won't hurt you. I would never want you to do anything that made you feel uncomfortable."

Grace almost jumped into his arms, almost let the tears fall. Instead, she took the last step until the front of her dress brushed against his coat.

He lowered his head, and she held her breath as his lips touched hers, so softly, so gently. The sensitive skin tingled as he brushed against her mouth, moving to rain faint kisses on her chin and along her jaw until she felt hot and dizzy.

The seductive smell of sandalwood swamped her, and she wondered if his skin tasted as divine. When he kissed her neck, she closed her eyes and let her head fall back.

"Elliot." The word left her lips between ragged breaths.

"Oh, God. Grace, I … I …"

She felt the sudden shift in him—his muscles growing harder, his breathing huskier. He brushed her lips again, firmer this time, his tongue penetrating her mouth with an urgency that shocked her.

A burning need emanated from him, the air about them thrumming with uncontrollable passion. All the wonderful feelings abandoned her as he crushed her to his chest. Panic took hold. And she struggled and writhed against him.

"No … let … let me go." She put her palms on his chest and pushed away from him.

"What's wrong?" He looked so tortured, so damnably handsome and confused.

Feelings of shame and mortification overpowered all else. What sort of woman struggled to kiss a man? Perhaps Henry was right. She was cold-hearted, unresponsive, lacked passion. When she thought of all the women eager to seduce Lord Markham, she felt so incapable, so inadequate.

"I'll meet you in the hall," she said, darting past him as she choked back a sob. But old habits drew her upstairs, and she ran into the room she'd slept in since her arrival, desperate to lock the door, desperate to lock him out.

He raced behind her, chasing her and she thought her heart would give way from the strain. When he caught her by the arm, she turned and screamed, "Please, Henry, don't."

"Grace. It is me. It's Elliot."

He pulled her into his arms as she tried to fight him.

"You're safe," he whispered, stroking her hair and holding her tight. "You're safe, Grace. It's Elliot. Henry is dead."

It took a moment for the words to penetrate her addled mind. Henry was dead, and she had acted like a fool. Too ashamed to look at Lord Markham, she wrapped her arms around his waist, took comfort in the warmth and security he provided.

"I'm sorry. I don't know what came over me."

"Hush. It doesn't matter," he said. "It's my fault."

She jerked away and forced herself to look at him. "No," she said, shaking her head vigorously. "You have done nothing wrong. It is me, Elliot. I am tainted by the memory of a monster."

He pulled her back into his chest and continued with his soothing ministrations. "You can trust me, Grace. We can be friends. I won't press you for anything more."

A feeling akin to grief flared. Friends would not be enough for her; she knew that now. "Give me another chance."

He kissed the top of her head. "Grace, I will give you anything you desire. But we cannot continue like this. You need to help me understand."

Sucking in a deep breath for courage, she nodded and stepped back. "Lie with me, Elliot. Just hold me in your arms, and I will tell you."

Mesmerising green eyes scanned the bed behind her. "This will be a first for me," he said with a smile as he took her hand and led her to the bed.

To know that he had never been this intimate with any other woman caused her heart to soar. She lay down next to him, let him gather her into his arms.

"I assume the monster you refer to is Henry?"

It was easier to talk about it in the dark. Being enveloped in a warm embrace gave her the strength to continue.

"Henry was to marry Caroline. He had loved her since they were children. But as the years passed it became more apparent that a provincial life was not for her." Grace placed her hand on his chest as it brought her comfort. "In his desperation, he did everything he could to persuade her to settle down with him. His parents made things increasingly more difficult for mine. When my father died, my mother was not strong enough to fight them."

Elliot stroked her hair, ran his hand down her back. "Are you saying you married a man you didn't love to help your sister and your mother?"

Grace swallowed deeply. It shocked her just how perceptive he was. It shamed her to admit she had been so naive.

"Henry thought that if he pressured me to marry him instead, as the eldest, Caroline would be forced to honour her responsibilities. Even in those final few minutes before we walked from the church as man and wife, I think he believed she would change her mind."

"Good heavens. Did you know he felt that way when you married him?"

"Of course not." Henry would have put Judas to shame. His kind and courteous nature masked the depth of his deceit. "I found this all out later. Indeed, Henry made it his mission to ensure I never forgot it. I think he punished me as a way of punishing Caroline."

Elliot gave a contemptuous snort. "But you never told her, did you? She came to London blissfully unaware of the devastation she had left behind."

"It wasn't her fault. It was mine. A cold-hearted devil tricked me into marriage. I was foolish enough to believe he cared. I thought it would be enough, that I would eventually grow to love him."

They lay in silence, but in her mind it sounded noisy and hectic.

Elliot turned onto his side to face her. "I am not Henry Denton, Grace. When I … when I kiss you it is my passion and desire for you that makes me so over-excited."

She glanced down at the gold buttons on his waistcoat. "Henry said I'm cold inside. He said I … I could never please a man."

Elliot took her chin between his thumb and finger, lifting her head until their gazes locked. "Grace, I have never met a more passionate woman. And it pleases me just being in your company."

His words went some way to heal her sad soul. She was tired of living in Henry's shadow. If she spent her whole life searching, she doubted she would ever find a gentleman as understanding as Elliot Markham. If she had any chance of putting the past behind her, she had to start now.

Grace placed her hand on his cheek and pressed her body closer to his. "Let me try again. Please, Elliot. I trust you. Just once. If it doesn't work, we'll be friends as you suggested."

He didn't answer. Not in words. Lowering his head towards her, he touched his lips to hers with a level of tenderness that stole her breath.

Desire unfurled like the petals of rosebuds in spring: slowly, curiously, with an element of wonder.

I have never met a more passionate woman.

A renewed sense of confidence burst forth. Was it his wonderful words spurring this change in her? Was it the fact she had bared her soul to him and survived?

In a bid to be nearer she shuffled closer, decided to kiss him in return. She brushed her mouth gently, tentatively across his. His unique scent surrounded her. She could taste it on his lips, the mix of raw masculinity and some wild, earthy essence she found intoxicating.

He let her set the pace. He lay there and let her kiss him softly and sweetly.

As a groan of appreciation rumbled in the back of his throat, she deepened the kiss, needing to satisfy a hunger clawing away inside. Her passion for him grew brighter and bigger. She traced the line of his lips with the tip of her tongue—to rouse a response, to let him know she was ready for more.

Elliot understood her silent plea. He wrapped his arms around her and pulled her on top of his hard body. His tongue met hers, caressing, dancing, delving deeper as his hands drifted lower to draw her against the evidence of his arousal.

"Grace," he whispered as they broke to catch their breath. He stared into her eyes. "Come home with me. Let me worship you in the only way I know how."

Excitement and fear fought a fierce internal battle. But her desire for him was too strong. In celebration, she kissed him deeply, passionately, her body writhing against his with a need she could not define.

She could hear their lustful pants, could feel a tightening deep in her core crying out to be appeased. She wanted to feel the warmth of his bare skin against hers, wanted to know if it was possible to feel pleasure when he moved inside her.

"Give me a little time. Tomorrow, I will stay with you tomorrow night."

"Only if you want to," he said, shuffling to sit upright.

She looked up at him. "I do want to." There was nothing she wanted more.

He glanced across to the window. "Perhaps it's as well. I cannot risk staying here. I need to make sure I'm home before sunrise."

She had forgotten all about his terrible affliction, and she scrambled from the bed. "Then we should be going. I would not want you to suffer on my account."

A sinful grin played at the corners of his mouth, and he crossed his arms behind his head. "We'll have a little time alone in my carriage. You can show me how grateful you are to me for offering my assistance. You can experiment on me with those delightful kisses I've suddenly grown so fond of."

Grace's heart soared. "I shall need a lot more practice, particularly with my tongue," she teased.

Elliot groaned. "You may use me as you wish. But be prepared. I may do some experimenting of my own."

CHAPTER 11

"It seemed more sensible for Elliot to lend us the use of his carriage," Evelyn said, glancing at Grace as they rattled along the busy streets. "The less time we spend out in public, the less chance we have of anyone identifying you."

Grace pursed her lips to suppress a grin. Being inside Elliot's conveyance roused memories of their journey home from Arlington Street. Just hours earlier she had sat astride him on the leather seat. Tempting him with her innocent kisses though they turned out to be not so innocent after all. The sound of his urgent pants and groans as she tugged at his hair had almost been her undoing, and she'd fought the need to lie back against the squab and offer herself to him.

"I don't care what people think of me," Grace said, feeling genuine affection for the lady who had kindly taken her into her home. "But I do worry about you."

Evelyn made a puffing sound. "In a few days, I shall be tucked away at Stony Cross and doubt I'll ever have cause to venture into town again. Let the gossips say what they will."

The carriage jerked to an abrupt halt amidst loud cries and protests.

Grace grabbed the edge of the seat. "It would have been

quicker to walk. With all the bleating outside it sounds as though we've been held up by a herd of sheep."

"Either that or the coachman has taken to impersonating farm animals."

Grace laughed. "Perhaps he is not used to escorting ladies about town and is trying his best to disguise his curses."

Evelyn smiled and after a brief silence suddenly said, "Elliot likes you. I think he likes you a great deal. Far more than he would care to admit."

The sudden change of topic startled her.

"He is just being kind," Grace said, her hand fluttering to her chest to calm her racing heart. The action was duly noted by her companion who gave another knowing grin. "I didn't really give him much choice in the matter."

"Kindness is the last trait others would associate with Elliot Markham. Even so, he has always been extremely kind and courteous to me. How he behaves around you, well, that is another matter entirely."

Grace tried to feign a nonchalant manner. But like a child in need of coddling, she wanted to indulge her fantasies. She wanted to believe the viscount held some affection for her.

"He treats me the same as he does everyone else." As soon as the words left her lips, she knew it wasn't really the case.

"No, he doesn't." Evelyn shook her head. "He treats you as though he is your protector. He looks at you as though you're a juicy piece of pie. He talks about you as though you are an angel sent down to cleanse him of his sins."

Grace swallowed deeply. Evelyn's honest opinion caused her stomach to perform a range of death-defying somersaults. "I find him the most honourable gentleman I have ever met," she said truthfully. She found him to be the most wickedly handsome, the most desirable gentleman of her acquaintance.

Evelyn gave a teasing smirk. "He must be very special to you for you to judge him so highly."

Grace considered her comment. He made her feel his equal in every way. He made her heart soar, soothed her soul. "He is."

They sat in silence. Her reply still echoed through her mind as Evelyn studied her with what could only be described as a look of excitement.

"And when you find your sister," Evelyn asked, "what then?"

Grace shrugged. She had not thought that far ahead. "We might not find her. But I will never stop looking. I can't think beyond that."

Evelyn offered her a compassionate smile. "We'll find her." She glanced out of the window. "Indeed, I believe we are stopping outside the apothecary."

As the carriage rolled to a halt, Elliot's footman opened the door and lowered the steps. "Wait for us on the corner of Swallow Street," Evelyn said. "We won't be more than twenty minutes."

The footman bowed and relayed the information to the coachman.

Grace studied the dark brown facade of the apothecary shop and noted the number forty-two painted in gold on the arch above the door.

"You seem disappointed." Evelyn cast a sidelong glance.

Grace shook her head. "I don't understand why Caroline would record something as insignificant as visiting an apothecary in her diary."

Evelyn threaded her arm through hers. "I'm sure it has more to do with who she was meeting and not where she was meeting them. We knew when we set out that it could be a wasted journey."

"Well, the only way to find out is to go inside," Grace said, trying to rouse some optimism.

A few people were milling about inside the shop. One gentleman sat in a chair in front of the counter while the apothecary, a painfully thin man with white hair, pounded away with his pestle and mortar grinding herbs into powder. The shelves behind him were brimming with a range of glass bottles containing a rainbow of coloured liquids.

On the opposite side, an assistant dispensed perfumes, soaps and balms.

"Let's try over here," Grace said, nodding to the perfumery counter. "Perhaps if I make a purchase, it will be easier to strike up a conversation."

The assistant acknowledged them immediately.

"I'm looking for sandalwood shaving soap," Grace said with a smile, aware of Evelyn's gaze shooting to her face.

"Certainly, madam. It is one of our most popular products." He scurried off to a cupboard and returned with a small earthenware pot.

Grace removed her glove, pulled off the lid and sniffed the contents. The intoxicating fragrance flooded her senses, rousing a memory of her inhaling Elliot's scent as she kissed along the line of his jaw.

"I would like two pots."

Evelyn tapped her on the arm. "Are you buying those for Elliot?"

She would give one pot to Elliot to thank him for his help. The other pot, well, she would look foolish if she said she planned to take one home to Cobham and so she simply nodded.

"That will be two shillings, madam."

A shilling for a small pot of shaving soap! No wonder he smelled so divine. It must surely contain only the finest ingredients.

Grace paid the assistant and used the opportunity to ask, "I had an appointment with Hodges last week, and I wondered if I could speak to him again."

"Shush." The assistant's frantic gaze shot left then right, and he tapped his finger to his lips twenty times or more. "You're not to mention it when there are customers in the shop." The man jerked his head back and blinked rapidly. "Did you just say *him*?"

Panic flared.

Grace's heart thumped hard in her chest. Judging by the man's wary expression, she had made a critical error. The only possible mistake was that Hodges was a woman.

"You must be mistaken." Grace offered her sweetest smile. "I'm sure I said *her*."

He raised his head in acknowledgement but did not appear entirely appeased. Offering a wide grin to the last customer leaving the shop, he turned and whispered, "Why do you want to see Mrs. Hodges?"

The hint of suspicion in his voice suggested that whatever services Mrs. Hodges provided, she did not run an altogether honest or lawful business. Grace feared opening her mouth as she had no idea how to answer.

"It is of a personal nature," Evelyn interrupted. She stepped closer to the counter. "It is a delicate situation."

The vague response had the desired effect, and the assistant nodded his head in recognition. "Give me a moment."

He walked over to the opposite side of the shop and muttered to the apothecary. The white-haired man removed his spectacles from the counter and balanced them precariously on the end of his nose. His suspicious gaze drifted over them. After a few moments, the man nodded and his assistant scuttled out through a door behind him.

Grace turned to Evelyn. "How did you know what to say?"

Evelyn shrugged. "I thought it covered a multitude of things."

"Well, it seemed to work."

The assistant returned. "Mrs. Hodges will see you now. You remember the way. It's through the door, up the stairs and the last door on the left." He glanced at Evelyn. "You're welcome to accompany your friend if you so wish."

Nerves caused Grace's muscles to stiffen. Acting as an

impostor and stepping into the unknown was something she should be used to after the events of the last few days.

Perhaps sensing her unease, the assistant leant across the counter. "The suppression pills contain only natural ingredients and offer no detriment to the constitution."

Suppression pills?

Grace had never heard of such a thing.

She smiled weakly. "Thank you. And my friend will join me."

The assistant held open the door and bowed graciously before closing it behind them. As they made their way upstairs, Evelyn touched her arm. "What on earth are suppression pills?"

Grace shook her head. "I haven't the faintest idea. Caroline must be suffering from an illness of some sort, although she seemed perfectly healthy to me. I recall mentioning how her complexion glowed."

"Well," Evelyn began as they approached the last door on the left. "There is only one way to find out."

Mrs. Hodges was a tall, lithe woman of middling years. She wore her hair tied loosely at her nape and her friendly, carefree manner put them instantly at ease. The furnishings in the small parlour were clean and comfortable; the sweet aromatic smells of numerous oils and herbs drifted up from the shop below to relax the senses. Grace and Evelyn were directed to the sofa while Mrs. Hodges sat in the chair opposite.

"Now. Before we begin, I must ask you how you knew to come here?" Mrs. Hodges said with a warm smile. "It is just a precaution. There's no need to be nervous."

Grace glanced at Evelyn. "We … I was told to come by a friend."

"Has your friend used my services before?"

"I believe so," Grace replied with a nod.

"Good. Then you know there is nothing to fear. You're here for the pills?"

"Yes," Grace replied, although she had no idea what that meant.

Evelyn shuffled forward. "Would you mind explaining a little more about it? My friend is far too nervous to ask."

"Of course." The woman inclined her head respectfully. "The pills work by removing impurities from the system, giving a new lease of energy and vitality. They have been used by women of the gentility and nobility in France for years."

Grace sighed inwardly. They were wasting their time here. If Caroline had come to see Mrs. Hodges, then it was for nothing more than a restorative.

"They work purely on the obstruction," she continued. "To re-establish the natural balance."

"Are there any risks involved?" Grace asked. The word *obstruction* niggled away in the back of her mind. The pills provided a means to rid the body of some sort of impediment. But why would Caroline be interested in that?

"They are risk-free. But are not to be taken if the lady is *enceinte.*"

Evelyn sucked in a breath. "And if the lady is with child and is unaware, what happens then?"

Mrs. Hodges' mouth formed a thin line. "Then the lady will suffer an expulsion."

"Expulsion?" Evelyn frowned.

Grace turned to her. "Mrs. Hodges means it will result in the loss of the child." As the words left her lips, she choked back a sob.

It all made more sense now. Caroline had invited her to stay with the intention of telling her something important. She was with child and had come to Mrs. Hodges to … to …

"I can see you need more time to consider your options," Mrs. Hodges said in a sympathetic tone. "The remedy is not suitable for everyone. With the obvious risk, it is not a decision to be made lightly."

"Thank you." Evelyn inclined her head as Grace struggled to speak. "We will not waste any more of your time."

The woman rose slowly from the chair and escorted them to the door. "If you decide to return, you must not leave it too long," she said, glancing down at Grace's stomach.

Grace nodded but could not raise a smile. To deny a child a chance of life was a criminal offence. No wonder the assistant had appeared a little frantic.

Once they had settled back into Elliot's carriage, she felt she could breathe a little easier.

"Do you believe your sister is with child?" Evelyn's voice sounded calm despite the gravity of the comment.

It was as though the dam suppressing all her feelings had suddenly collapsed under the pressure, and a torrent of emotion burst forth.

"Oh, Evelyn. She must have been utterly desperate to visit such an awful place. Why didn't she tell me sooner? I could have helped her. We could have talked it through. What if she has taken those terrible pills and something has gone wrong? What if she's lying somewhere, so cold, so alone?"

Evelyn crossed the carriage to sit at her side. She took Grace's hand and cupped it between her own. "Think about it, Grace. Mrs. Hodges didn't recognise you. She did not even give you a second glance. She made no mention of you having been there before, or that you looked remotely familiar. If Caroline had bought any of those pills, surely Mrs. Hodges would have made the usual assumption and asked how you fared with them."

Grace swallowed and tried to calm her racing heart. "You mean Caroline may have changed her mind?"

"Perhaps she acted on impulse. Perhaps she arranged to go there but couldn't go through with it."

Grace looked down to her lap. Caroline never faltered once her mind was made up. "We are no closer to finding her than we were an hour ago."

"No, but it is all starting to make a little more sense now. I think we need to concentrate on who could have fathered the child. Who was her latest beau? Who paid the rent on her house in Arlington Street?"

Evelyn made it all sound so simple.

"And how are we supposed to do that?" Grace implored.

"We will discuss it with Alexander and Elliot. But I suggest you stop pretending that you're Caroline. I suggest we go out into Society and tell everyone you're her sister. You're a widow. No one will question your friendship with Elliot."

"But what will that achieve?"

"People love nothing more than gossip." Evelyn patted her hand. "I expect you will hear all sorts of tales about your sister, some complete and utter lies but some truths, too."

"I do think Lady Sudley's behaviour odd. I should like the opportunity to talk to her again."

Evelyn smiled. "That settles it then. I shall speak to Alexander and arrange for invitations to the most popular event this evening. With us being so recently wed, every hostess in London is happy to extend their hospitality to the new Lady Hale."

A stab of guilt hit her in the chest. "I'm sorry you're embroiled in all of this."

"Don't be. We would do anything for Elliot, and we will do anything for you."

Grace squeezed her hand. "Then I will need to call at Arlington Street to find something suitable to wear. And I should go and speak to Elliot and tell him what we have discovered."

"Would you mind dropping me off at Duke Street? Alexander will be pacing the floor wondering what's happened, and I may have to make a few calls."

"Of course." Grace nodded. "I won't be too long."

"Take as long as you need," she said, offering a knowing grin. "I won't expect you back for hours."

The suggestive tone caused Grace's heart to skip a beat. She would call and see Elliot, just to tell him the news. But then her mind decided to conjure an image of his soft lips, and the smell of sandalwood filled her head to tease and torment her.

When it came to Elliot Markham, she could not control the wild nature of her thoughts. Someone once told her that if you thought about something for long enough it would eventually come true. And so she spent the next few minutes dreaming about his sinful mouth, hoping his masterful hands held the magical ability to banish the ghosts of the past.

CHAPTER 12

Elliot lay sprawled on his bed, his head cushioned by a mound of pillows. For the umpteenth time since returning home in the small hours, he imagined punching Alexander Cole until he had no fight left in him.

His fingers throbbed in frustration, which was a damn sight better than the throbbing ache currently plaguing his cock.

Before making Alexander's acquaintance, he had wandered aimlessly from one social gathering to another, looking for a way to relieve the boredom. Bedding women suppressed his ennui. His indifference served to punish the fair sex for the crimes of one golden-haired devil and one equally cold-hearted mother. It proved he did not deserve the love of a decent woman.

Now, everything had changed. He had to blame someone for his unstable emotions. Why not Alexander? The gentleman's caring gestures and soft words of endearment had penetrated Elliot's hardened heart. Indeed, one could not witness his obsession with his wife and not feel slightly envious.

One thing was certain. In Grace Denton's company he was not himself. Never had he taken a woman in his arms while still fully clothed. Nor had he felt the strange churning in his stomach when she'd rebuked his advances and darted from the kitchen up to her chamber.

She did make amends, though, by indulging in a rather salacious kiss in his carriage. It boded well for their joining. A deep, intense passion burned just beneath the surface, and he knew he possessed the skills necessary to release it.

Perhaps once he'd bedded her, these strange feelings would subside. Perhaps then he could get back to a semblance of normalcy. It was easy to convince himself he felt nothing more than physical desire when he wasn't staring into those perfect blue eyes or offering tender words of comfort.

The light rap at the door disturbed his reverie.

"Mrs. Denton is here, my lord," Whithers said solemnly. "I know you do not like to be disturbed, but she assured me it was important."

No doubt it related to her snooping expedition to Piccadilly.

"You may show her up," he replied. With the sun still high, he was safe in his chamber—as long as Grace didn't open the drapes.

When she breezed into his chamber, he stood to greet her. While a prisoner in his room, his affliction didn't render him an invalid.

"My lord. Forgive me barging in here when you're resting," she said, her gaze drifting over his relaxed attire. He wore trousers, his shirt hanging loose and open at the neck yet she appeared more interested in his bare feet. "You have nice feet."

He couldn't help but chuckle at the odd remark. "As opposed to ugly ones?"

She waved her hand in the air. "Your toes follow a perfect arch and as such are more pleasing to the eye. It means you descend from the ancient Egyptians."

Elliot felt the same deep level of intimacy he always experienced in her company. Yet it only bothered him when he tried to examine and analyse the emotion. "Then I'm pleased. The Egyptians are a proud and noble race." He glanced down to the kid boots peeking out from beneath her walking dress. "But now I am curious to know from where you descend."

She gave him a coy smile. The brightness warmed his heart and made his cock twitch. "All in good time. The thrill of anticipation is a wonderful thing."

He imagined taking each one of her pretty white toes into his mouth and sucking softly.

Bloody hell.

He needed to calm his racing pulse before he tore the clothes from her body in his eagerness to be near her.

"Would you care to sit?" He gestured to the seating area in front of the fire, and she shrugged out of her pelisse, removed her bonnet and gloves and placed them on the side table. "I can ring Whithers to bring refreshment if you'd care for tea?"

"No. I'm fine," she said, shuffling back in the chair as she patted down the stray strands of hair. "But if you need blood, then please do not wait for me."

There had been moments in the last four years where he had imagined being open about his horrendous affliction. Grace did not understand the full depth of his depravity. Would she think differently if she knew a woman had infected him? Would she think differently if she knew it was not an illness but an evil curse?

"Did you visit the shop in Piccadilly?" he said, dropping into the chair opposite.

"You were right. It is an apothecary." She gave a sorrowful sigh. "For a moment, I'd almost forgotten how dreadful the morning has been."

Elliot sat forward. "Dreadful? How so?"

He had persuaded himself it was nothing to do with him if she chose to go gallivanting about town. While no one could deny desire sparked between them, there were no promises made, no expectations. However, he could not hide the sudden shot of panic.

Grace thrust forward, the movement surprising him. "Oh, Elliot. Caroline is with child. I'm convinced of it."

"With child?" he repeated for fear he'd misheard. "You discovered that at the apothecary?"

"The Hodges mentioned in her diary is a Mrs. Hodges. She has a room above the shop. I think she is related to the proprietor and sells suppression pills which …" Grace swallowed deeply, and he noticed her bottom lip quiver. "If taken, they can cause the loss of a child."

Sitting back in his chair, he dragged his palm down his face. He had heard of such things before. When one had a relaxed attitude to sexual liaisons, it was to be expected.

Elliot did not have to worry about fathering a child. His affliction rendered him incapable.

The taunts and jibes of the golden-haired devil left a permanent imprint in his mind. Even when he had bowed his head and refused to look at her, still she yanked him up by his hair and continued to berate him.

Feeling a burning need to rid himself of the memory, he shook his head and tried to concentrate on the kind, beautiful lady in front of him.

"You don't know if she has taken these pills," he said in an attempt to offer comfort.

"Evelyn thinks Mrs. Hodges would have noticed the similarity between us. The fact she made no mention of it could mean Caroline changed her mind."

Elliot nodded. "It is a possibility." He did not wish to predict the workings of a woman's mind. And with Grace's thoughts being so abstract he could not tune into them, either.

"Evelyn said we need to find out who fathered the child, and who pays the rent on Caroline's house. She thinks I need to let people know who I really am. She's going to secure invitations to the most popular balls." She was speaking so quickly he had to concentrate just to make sense of it all. "When people learn

I'm Caroline's sister, we hope the gossips will be eager to offer information."

"Well. You've certainly been busy." He did not know which part of the plan to protest against first. "Do you think it wise to reveal your identity? Once this matter is settled, you may wish to come to town on occasion."

Her eyes grew wide, the corners of her mouth turning down in disdain. "I hate it here. The ballrooms are packed with fakes and frauds. They are full of people who hide behind a feigned persona, who wander around looking for others to tickle their fancy."

Elliot folded his arms across his chest. "You'll find that wherever you go. It is the way of the world."

"It is not my way."

For some reason, her comment roused his ire. Was she judging him?

"Forgive me for being blunt, but did you not construct a feigned persona when you married Henry Denton? You were hardly true to yourself then."

Her expression grew solemn, the brilliant light banished from her countenance. She bit down on her bottom lip before sucking in a breath. "It is hardly the same. I believed he cared. What I did, I did for the sake of others, not out of vanity or some over-inflated notion of my own worth."

"Does being a martyr make you any less a fool?"

As soon as the words tumbled from his pathetic mouth, he wished he could reclaim them. If he'd ripped the dress from her back and administered twenty lashes, the look she cast him would have been equally the same. His words must have cut deep, deep enough to draw blood.

"You think me a fool?" She stood abruptly. "I can see you hide the Devil's own tongue behind your godly persona. It is obvious you do not understand me at all, so I shall say good day to you, my lord."

She swung around, knocked into the arm of the chair. Despite offering a groan, she marched towards the door.

In any other situation, with any other woman, he would have opened the door and shouted good riddance. But it pained him to think she harboured ill feeling towards him. It pained him to think he would never know if their joining would be different from the whole host of other women he'd bedded.

Most disturbing of all, he did not want to hurt her. He wanted her to look upon him as her hero, her champion in her fight against the enemy.

He wanted Grace Denton to love him.

Bloody hell!

He flew out of the chair, tried to shake away the last thought. As her hand gripped the handle, he rushed over to her, trapped her against the door with his body. Determined to convince himself his lustful loins had concocted the last thought, he focused on persuading her to stay.

"Forgive me," he whispered against her hair.

In her rush to leave, it occurred to him she had left her pelisse and bonnet on the table. She would have had to come back. If only he had waited. It would have saved him the humiliation of sounding so desperate.

"Why?" she muttered.

"I spoke out of turn. I did not mean it in the way you think." He inhaled the sweet smell of orange blossom; he let the heat from her body warm him. If he had his way, he'd bunch her dress up to her waist and take her there and then. Hard and quick against the door—to prove it would be the same as it had always been. To prove he would feel nothing.

But as she turned to face him, the pain in her eyes tore at his soul.

Her gaze drifted over his face and dropped to the opening of his shirt. "Why do I feel like hitting you and kissing you both at the same time?"

Relief flashed through him.

"You may hit me if you wish. As long as you kiss me with the same fiery passion."

What happened next would remain with him until the moment he took his last breath. As they stared into each other's eyes, he felt her hands move up under his shirt, felt tentative fingers brush over the muscles in his abdomen. When they moved up to his chest, he could hear the hitch in his breath, could feel desire burn through his body until he was ready to combust.

Take it slow, be gentle.

The words echoed through the chambers of his mind to calm the ravaging fire tearing through his veins.

Damn it. At this rate, he'd struggle to last more than a minute.

He always felt an urgent need to rush the act, to race towards the moment of freedom, to experience the intense euphoria that accompanied his release.

For the first time in his life he would need to relinquish control. He stepped back, felt the loss of her warm hands instantly.

"Grace … I want you more than I have ever wanted anything." He sounded nothing like himself. He was panting, struggling with his words, could hear his heartbeat thudding in his ears. "But I do not want to rush you."

A smile played at the corners of her mouth. "I've decided to do things differently. I've decided to kiss you first and hit you later."

Her blue eyes were softer, revealing the depth of her desire.

"I need you to set the pace," he said. "Do what you will with me, without fear."

Panic flashed in her eyes. "I'm not good at this." She waved her hand back and forth between them. "I won't know how to please you."

They stood there like virgins on their wedding night: fully

clothed, shaking, neither one knowing what the hell to do next. As the gentleman, he would have to do something.

"Trust me," he said, pulling his shirt over his head and throwing it to the floor. "Anything you do to me will be more than pleasing."

His words seemed to give her confidence, but her gaze drifted down his chest, past the faint red marks that were still healing, to the branding mark of the Devil.

"What's that?" She ran her fingers around the circle of barbed twine. "Is it a holy symbol?"

He almost laughed out loud. She was referring to the cross in the centre, of course. "It is a branding mark. I shall tell you about the scar later. But for now, can we focus on the removal of your garments?"

His distraction technique worked, and her eyes widened in response. "What? All of them?"

"Of course. Grace, I want to bathe in the splendour of your naked body. I want to feel the warmth of your skin pressed against mine."

"Oh."

Perhaps Henry Denton preferred to take her under the coverlet, with her dressed in a thick cotton nightgown.

Damn. He did not want to think about her in bed with another man. "I suggest you kiss me now then we will work towards the goal of freeing us both of all restrictions."

The corners of her mouth crept up into a sinful smile. "I think I have mastered the kissing part. It's up to you to help me master the rest." She stepped towards him, her hands coming to rest on his chest.

"Show me what you've mastered," he said, his cock straining against the fabric of his trousers.

She pressed her lips to his, softly at first. As her hands moved up to caress the muscles in his shoulders and neck, a seductive sigh breezed across his mouth.

"Close your eyes," she whispered, and he obliged. "I want

you to show me how to worship your body, Elliot." The words drifted over his neck. The fine hairs at his nape tingled in response.

The anticipation was like nothing he had felt before.

Every part of him ached for her.

Every part of him shook with a need he could not define.

"I'll show you everything," he replied. As his lips formed the last word, she covered them with her own, her tongue penetrating his mouth so sweetly.

That's when it hit him.

With Grace, everything felt different.

With Grace, everything felt wonderful and new.

CHAPTER 13

Despite charging to the door in anger and telling herself she didn't need Elliot Markham in her life, Grace kissed him as though his mouth provided everything she needed to breathe, to exist.

This addiction she had for him, for his taste, his smell, for the deep groans resonating from the back of his throat, controlled her thoughts and actions.

She tried to suppress her feelings.

Nothing good could come of it. Not in the long term. But the part of her that wanted to experience real pleasure, the part that wanted to forget Henry Denton, would take this wonderful man as her lover regardless of the consequences.

Even the fear she'd once felt clawing away inside had been trampled down by her overwhelming need for him.

Perhaps it had something to do with the fact she felt in control. Elliot did not dominate, mistreat or abuse her.

The thought caused a rush of emotion to flood her chest, and she deepened the kiss in response, pressing her body closer to his in the process. Until now, he had played a secondary role in this melding of mouths. But as her eager hands scrambled over the hard muscles in his arms and back to ease the ache deep in her core, he responded by swinging her around and fiddling frantically with the buttons on the back of her dress.

"I can't touch you with all of these layers," he complained, and he did not see the smile that touched her lips.

"Can you manage?"

He gave an arrogant snort as his hands brushed the sleeves from her shoulders and the material sank to the floor with ease. He clasped her elbow as she stepped out of the fabric pool.

"I'll leave the rest for a minute," he said, pulling her into an embrace. He bent his knees as he claimed her mouth, letting his hands ride up underneath her petticoat and chemise.

The light touch of his fingers gliding over her bare legs caused a bolt of desire to shoot through her body. The throbbing sensation between her thighs cried out for his touch.

"Let me ease your suffering," he whispered against her mouth as if he could read her thoughts, interpret her movements. His hot palms moulded around her buttocks. "Tell me," he continued, nuzzling her neck. "Do you cry out in your release or do you pant and moan?"

His lips left a molten trail in their wake, and she swallowed before finding the breath to speak. "My … my release?" she asked with some confusion as her head fell back and another wave of pleasure pulsed through her. "I do-don't know what you mean."

He stopped suddenly and searched her face. A sinful grin formed. "You don't know what I mean?" He seemed pleased with her answer. "Oh, then you are in for a real treat."

Without another word he went to work on the hook and eye clasps, on the ties of her stays, removing her plain linen chemise until she stood before him, naked and exposed.

He stepped back and surveyed her form as though she were an exhibit of fine art. When he clasped his hand over his mouth, she feared there was something wrong. Henry had refused to look at her like this, and she had a sudden urge to clutch her clothing to her chest and hang her head in shame.

"Wh-what's wrong?" she found the courage to say, moving her arms to cover her breasts.

"Wrong? Why would you think there's anything wrong?" He took her hands in his and held them out wide as his hungry eyes devoured every inch of her. "You're perfect. Perfect for me. Perfect in every way. And your breasts, well, the word *spectacular* springs to mind."

Her cheeks burned. She found she admired him a little more for the compliment.

If only she'd met him a year ago.

"Come," he said, taking her hand and guiding her towards the bed. "There is something we must rectify before we can continue."

Curiosity burned away inside. "Now I'm intrigued," she said, her husky tone revealing her desire.

Elliot touched his lips to hers, pulled her to his hard body and moved so her breasts rubbed against the dusting of hair on his chest. The muscles deep in her core pulsed again. As their tongues became lost in each other's mouths, he lowered her down to the bed.

He came down on top of her and the slightest frisson of fear resurfaced. What if she felt squashed? What if she felt as though all the air was being squeezed from her lungs? Panic would set in. She would be plagued by nightmares of Henry.

She pushed at Elliot's chest, and he raised himself up on his arms. "Your trousers," she said by way of a distraction, just to give her a moment to catch her breath. "You need to remove them."

"In a moment. I won't hurt you, Grace. I'm about to show you how much I want you." He cast her a wicked smile, and her heart melted. All negative thoughts subsided.

Perhaps he sensed her fear, could hear her thoughts.

Plundering her mouth with a swift but wildly erotic kiss, he moved to rain featherlight kisses down her neck, moving lower still.

Her heart thumped loudly in her chest when he took her nipple into his mouth, teasing it to peak. The fluttering sensation travelled down to her toes. Grace threw her head back and closed her eyes to stave off her embarrassment.

But then he moved lower still, his tongue dipping into and circling her navel as he hooked his arms under her knees and bent her legs.

She was exposed to him now, laid open and bare. "Elliot, don't look. I … I can't …"

"Hush," he whispered. "Trust me."

When his mouth moved against her most intimate place, she gasped for breath, clutched at the coverlet. But he continued to torment her, sucking, licking and kissing, the tip of his tongue penetrating her entrance.

She should have felt shame. She should have tried to stop him.

But it felt so wonderful, so utterly divine.

Elliot lavished her with attention until her breathing grew raspy, until her mind grew foggy and she struggled to rouse a coherent thought. Her body tingled in response. The muscles in her core tightened. She reached down, grabbed his hair and rubbed brazenly against his mouth.

She heard a distant hum of pleasure. Whether it came from his throat or hers, she didn't know, and she could feel herself being drawn towards a magical abyss.

It came upon her swiftly. The waves of intense pleasure rushed through her entire body. She writhed and moaned against him, called his name. The muscles in her core spasmed, clamped down around his tongue as he thrust it inside her shamelessly.

"*Elliot. Oh, I … I …*"

Her legs shook. She arched her back, surrendered to the strange yet glorious sensation rippling through her, lifting her from the bed and carrying her away to a heavenly place.

Feeling giddy and a little disorientated, she lay there until she found the courage to open her eyes.

Elliot raised his head, an arrogant smile playing at the corners of his mouth. "Now I'll remove my trousers."

Unbuttoning and sliding out of them with speed and efficiency he threw them to the floor, and she gasped again at the sight of his jutting erection.

If she told him that she'd never seen a man naked before, he would think it absurd. But as she stared and marvelled in wonder, she knew he could see the truth.

"Touch me," he said, coming to lie at her side. "Let me feel your soft hand wrapped around me."

Grace swallowed as nerves tried to push to the fore. But she was still soaring on the dizzying heights of her release. With trembling fingers she reached out and touched him, growing instantly aroused by the sheer strength and power emanating from within. His skin felt smooth, like a veil of silk shrouding a rod of solid iron and his growl of appreciation gave her the courage she needed.

As he lay back on the bed, she rolled onto her side and studied his reactions to try to find the right rhythm. She stroked him, pulling the skin taut to expose the glistening head. Grace wondered what it would be like to take him in her mouth, and her mind became distracted imagining the taste and sensation.

"Next time," he panted as he covered her hand. "I want you now, Grace."

As she rolled onto her back and his magnificent, sculptured body covered hers, she prepared herself to feel the heavy weight of him pressing her down into the mattress. But his mouth settled on her nipple, lavished them both with equal attention until she was writhing beneath him once more.

Lost in rapturous ecstasy, she'd not noticed him shift position, not until he pushed slowly inside her.

In one long fluid movement he stretched her, filled her deep. She grasped his firm buttocks and revelled in the slow grinding movements that sent bolts of pleasure shooting to her core. Elliot quickened the pace, thrust hard as he angled his hips. The motion brought with it the tightening feeling in her abdomen. Only now, she could feel it in every part of her body. Now the muscles clamped around him, squeezing and pulsating, drawing him deeper.

"*Elliot*."

They were panting, groaning, gasping for breath. She wrapped her legs tightly around him, anchoring him to her. Not wanting to let him go. Sweat trickled down his back. She dug her fingers into the muscled planes, pressed her body close to his as she knew he would soon withdraw.

"Grace … I … holy hell."

He slowed his pace and closed his eyes, his face revealing the pleasure he gleaned from the last few strokes. When he collapsed on top of her, breathless and exhausted, she didn't feel squashed or overwhelmed. She felt happy. Yet her mind soon became occupied with a host of thoughts and feelings.

Their joining had been like nothing she had ever experienced before. Fragments of desire still pulsed through her body. She felt connected to Elliot in a way she never thought possible. He had not only claimed her body, but she feared he had claimed her heart and soul, too.

One terrifying question consumed her. Why had he not withdrawn?

"Now do you know what I mean when I promised you release?" he said, drawing her closer to his warm body and rolling onto his side, despite the fact he was still buried inside her. "I assume you found it pleasurable?"

She cuddled into him as a way of banishing all worries from her mind temporarily. "I feel wonderful. I did not know it was possible to experience such a thing."

He chuckled. "You writhe in such a seductive way, and the sweetest moans escape from your lips. It is a wonderful sight to behold."

"As is your face. It lit up the whole room." Knowing she had no option but to ask the next question, she caressed his chest as a distraction. "You know when you want to prevent … when you don't want—"

"I am incapable of fathering a child, Grace," he said as he eased himself out of her and rolled onto his back. "I've been told it is a consequence of my affliction."

A hard lump formed in her throat. It took a moment for her to determine why.

She wanted him, for now, for always. But she wanted children.

"Will it always be that way?" she said, and her voice sounded a little solemn.

"I'm afraid there is no cure. Of that I am certain."

An icy chill breezed over her and she shivered. Was there more to this illness than what he'd told her?

"You're cold," he continued. "Let's slide under the sheets, and we'll soon have you warm again."

She studied his face. It was difficult to know what he was thinking. "You want to stay in bed for a while?"

"I do." He sounded just as surprised.

Perhaps it was time to touch upon another of her fearful thoughts.

"Is it wise? I … I heard you never touch the same lady twice."

He stared into her eyes, brushed her hair from her face. "For you, I will make an exception."

CHAPTER 14

Elliot pulled back the sheets, and they climbed into bed. He was still trying to come to terms with the fact he wanted her again. Now. He wanted to hear her little pants and moans. He wanted to feel her essence surround him, wanted to feel the same bone-shattering release he'd felt moments earlier.

When she propped herself up on her elbow and her sapphire-blue eyes studied his face, he knew the question she would ask before her lips formed the words.

"How did you come by this terrible affliction? If it is not contagious, how is it Alexander has it, too?"

He contemplated lying to her. But knowing Evelyn, she may have already told her about the golden-haired temptress. Besides, Grace had confided in him, confessed to her mistakes.

She would not judge him.

Elliot closed his eyes and inhaled deeply. He couldn't do it. He couldn't let the words leave his lips. They lay buried beneath a veil of arrogance that had taken years to perfect, buried so deep they were almost lost to him.

"It is complicated," he said in an attempt to placate her.

"You do not have to tell me anything, Elliot. But you can trust me with your secret."

In the last four years, he had never considered telling anyone about his affliction. If he waited for an eternity, he doubted he would find anyone else he could confide in.

"It is not a disease, Grace," he suddenly said, a little shocked at how easily he had submitted. "It is the Devil's curse. The story of how I came by it is far worse than any nightmare."

A frown marred her pretty brow. "A curse? You're not serious?"

"I have never been more serious about anything."

"Someone cursed you?"

Elliot swallowed. "Someone bit me. Transferred their evil poison into my blood."

"Bit you!" She put her hand to her throat. "But why?"

It was a question he had spent long, torturous hours deliberating. "I have no idea. I have asked myself the same question a hundred times, and there is only one feasible answer—revenge."

Her eyes grew wide. "You know the person who did this to you?"

He struggled to raise a smile. "No. I do not know her. But she had a look in her eyes, a hatred for men. She also bit Alexander and Leo—"

"Your friend, the Turkish prince," she gasped, "he suffers with it, too?"

"We were bitten at different times, in different locations, although all within miles of her home it seems."

"But if you do not know her, why would she mark you as the object to satisfy her need for revenge?"

Elliot brushed his hand through his hair. "The only commonality we shared is that we were all libertines. We all used women for our own pleasure without thought or feeling."

Grace raised a brow. "Were libertines?" The words carried a hint of contempt mingled with disbelief.

"I refuse to change my ways because some golden-haired temptress ruined my life in a fit of rage. I refuse to let her beat me. I refuse to let her win."

A look of sadness swamped her countenance. "But have you won, Elliot? Does refusing to show any emotion truly make you the victor?"

"I show emotion with you," he said, acknowledging she was not simply another woman he used to ease his boredom.

"Of course," she replied, although he sensed her doubt, her lack of confidence in him. "Do you still see her?"

Elliot sighed as he stared up at the ceiling. "I have not laid eyes on her for four years. Not since that fateful night in Bavaria."

"Bavaria?"

She fell silent for a moment. He took comfort from the feel of her full breasts pushing against his ribs. In the past, whenever he thought of the dreadful night he turned from human to demon, he'd look to his ravenous appetite to numb the pain. Until today, he had not cared where he put his cock.

"Tell me about the night you met her." Grace ran her hand over his chest, the motion soft and soothing. Her tone held a rich, seductive quality and he wondered if she had her own form of mind magic. "Tell me all the things you've never dared to tell another."

The rhythmical sensation relaxed him; soon his mind drifted back to the night Satan's disciple stole his humanity, stole his soul.

"I remember it was raining, although the sky appeared clear and I recall looking up and wondering what had happened to the dark clouds. I see it now as an omen, a warning of what was to come."

He sighed deeply. What he would give to feel the rain on his face again. What he would give to make a different decision, take a different path.

"It all started a couple of days before. I'd been drinking in a tavern with a lady I'd met earlier in the day," he began. "Her husband had been drinking with us, too. But he drank quickly, two drinks to every one of mine. When his head hit the table, he began to snore, and we laughed. She told me she admired me, told me I could have her if I were quick about it. She was older, yet still possessed a certain charm I could not refuse."

"It didn't matter to you that she was married?" He could hear her disappointment.

"No, Grace. It didn't matter." Now he'd started his story the words poured out like water through a breach in a dam; he decided he'd tell her everything. "There was an old graveyard just a short walk from the tavern. Rows of grey, dusty mausoleums lined the cobbled walkways to the east. Each stone building was littered with tall spires shaped in various images of a cross, stretching up so high the tops prodded the inky sky. To the west, there were tombs surrounded by iron railings, graves with broken headstones."

He fell silent not knowing if he could continue.

"Did you take the lady from the tavern there that night?" Her voice sounded softer now as she tried to help him finish his story.

"That night and the night after."

He knew what she was thinking. Before he'd turned, he had no problem taking the same woman twice.

"On the third night, things were different. I felt a heaviness in the air, an intense pressure, which I put down to a fear of her husband waking from his drunken slumber. I … I heard a voice in my head calling out to me, an ominous warning. But my desire to have the woman again obliterated everything else. We followed the same routine as the previous two nights, went inside the open mausoleum where it was dry, a little warmer." He dragged his gaze away from the spot on the ceiling and turned to look at her. "You do not want to hear any more of this, Grace."

She gave a weak smile. "I think you need to tell someone about it. You have buried your feelings, Elliot. You have feigned indifference, but whatever happened that night has affected you deeply."

"Perhaps. Though it is easier not to think of it."

"I know. But I'm here for you. You must continue."

He believed she did know what it felt like to have lived through a nightmare; she still carried scars, too.

"I had barely even begun when the lady from the tavern thrust her hand to her throat as she suddenly struggled and gasped for breath. Her eyes grew wide, fat and round, almost bulging from their sockets. Then, as quick as it had started, she could breathe easily again. Panic flashed in her eyes and she muttered to herself, answering silent questions. Then she turned and fled."

"What did you do?"

"I stood there, shocked and confused. I heard the voice in my head and then a woman appeared in the doorway, the hood of her travelling cloak pulled up to hide her face. In the small confines of the tomb, she seemed to have some strange power over me. Her soothing voice sent me to sleep like a babe rocked to the hum of a sweet melody."

"Was that the woman who bit you?"

"Yes, but I only have a vague recollection of it. When I woke, my clothes had been stripped from my back, my arms held wide by iron chains threaded through metal rings in the wall. 'You are my slave now,' she said. 'You are a slave to your own passions, a slave to the night.'"

"A slave to the night?" Grace frowned.

"She spent what seemed like days taunting and tormenting me, telling me all about the monster I was to become, although I know we could not have been there for more than a few hours. After she'd sunk her teeth into my neck, I must have lost consciousness."

Grace looked horrified. "What happened when you woke?"

"I thought I'd been dreaming." He couldn't help but snort as he recalled feeling an overwhelming sense of relief. "But then I noticed the branding mark burnt into my chest and when I tried to leave the mausoleum, the sun scorched my skin. I fed for the first time that night." He exhaled deeply and blinked rapidly to block it all out. "It was a long time ago. I have managed to find a way to reclaim some semblance of a life."

Grace placed her head on his chest, and while they lay in silence, the devil's taunts occupied his thoughts.

No one would want him. No one could ever care for a blood-thirsty beast.

"I think we both need to put the past behind us," she said, the tip of her finger tracing the mark seared into his skin as a permanent reminder. "It's easier for me. My scars do not impact daily life as drastically as yours. But perhaps sharing the burden makes it more bearable."

"You can move on, Grace. You can have a happy life. Who would want to share in my burden or my life? Who would want to live with a man who hides a murderous monster within?"

"Someone who loves you. Someone whose life would be meaningless without you."

He swallowed as fear and hope flooded his chest, the conflicting emotions fighting for supremacy. "I have never been a dreamer," he said, as his fear announced itself the victor. "I prefer to find a way to numb all painful memories."

He tried to listen to her thoughts, but his own mind struggled to focus.

"Well, I am here for you," she said. Her hand drifted down over his chest, over the muscles in his abdomen. "You have helped me more than you will ever know. Someone had stolen the light from within. You have found it, restored it. In time, I am confident it will shine brightly again."

He leant closer and kissed her forehead. In all the years, during all his licentious encounters, he had never kissed any other woman in so intimate, so caring a way.

"I want to do something for you," she continued. "I want to help numb your pain."

He gave a weak chuckle. "Grace, you have just given me more than I could ever have hoped."

She rolled on top of him, her soft breasts brushing against his chest as she shimmied down under the sheets. “With your help, with your expert tuition, I am sure there is more I can give.”

Leaving a trail of hot, wet kisses in her wake, she threw back the covers and knelt between his legs. The glorious sight alone was almost his undoing. He could sense her nerves, appreciated the selflessness of the act.

It made the experience all the more magnificent, all the more memorable, all the more meaningful.

CHAPTER 15

"When we looked through our correspondence, we found we had already been invited," Evelyn said as they made their way into the Croxtons' ballroom. "It only took a little gentle persuasion for Lady Croxton to extend the invitation to visiting guests."

"She did look at me rather strangely when I entered the receiving line," Grace said. "I'm certain she thinks I'm Caroline and have given a false name with the intention of ruining her soiree."

Evelyn leant closer. "Either way, it gives the gossiping birds a fat juicy worm to feed on."

Grace felt a sudden tickle in her tummy when Elliot moved to her side and put his hand to the small of her back, and she turned to face him.

"Would you care for some refreshment?" His vibrant green eyes sparkled as his gaze dropped to her mouth. "I believe you may have worked up quite a thirst this afternoon."

She liked the way his face lit up when he smiled as opposed to the look of pain and anguish she had witnessed earlier.

"I am in need of something to wet my lips," she replied brazenly in a bid to prolong the intimacy of the moment.

"I am brimming with suggestions." His sinful gaze fell to the exposed curve of her breasts. "But for now, it is best to settle for a glass of lemonade." Leaning closer, he whispered, "I should like you moist and hydrated when I take you home tonight."

Desire pulsed through her just thinking about all they had shared. The few hours she had spent in his chamber had altered her in some way. She felt stronger. Alive. Free.

"Why wait until then?"

Elliot laughed. The sound was music for her soul. "I fear I shall never be able to beat you when it comes to salacious banter."

"Good. I would hate you to find me tiresome."

"Tiresome?" He raised a brow. "I find you exactly the opposite."

Alexander stepped forward and jerked his head in the direction of the hallway. "Come. Let us leave the ladies to mingle and gossip. Remember we have but a few hours to gather as much information as we can."

Elliot bowed to her. "I shall return soon with your refreshment, my lady."

Grace gave an amused smile. "Hurry," she said, aware of the numerous gazes directed her way. "I fear the vultures are circling. You may return to find nothing more than a pile of scraggy bones."

"Then I'm thankful I had the foresight to enlist help. Leo has been feeling a little unwanted of late. The ladies will stop at nothing to keep his attention and he does so like to gossip." Elliot turned and scanned the sea of heads. "He's here somewhere. With strict instructions to learn as much as he can about Caroline Rosemond."

Just from the way he spoke, it was obvious Elliot felt a certain responsibility towards his friend. Perhaps when one shared such a terrible affliction, it was only natural for a strong bond to develop. And it pleased her to know he had someone else who understood the weight of his burden.

“Excellent.” She beamed. “The more, the merrier. I don’t think I could face another night of fancy frocks and packed ballrooms.”

His gaze dropped again to the scandalously low neckline of yet another one of Caroline’s gowns. “If they’re all like that one, I think I could happily face a hundred or so such nights.”

“Off with you,” she said, shooing him away before she gave in to temptation and threw her arms around his neck. “I’m supposed to be here to help Caroline, and you’re too much of a distraction.”

“I’ll give you twenty minutes and then I’m coming back to distract you even more.”

She watched him push through the crowd, her thoughts turning warm and dreamy as she imagined how wonderful it would be to lie next to him in bed each night.

Evelyn clutched Grace’s arm and gave it an affectionate squeeze. “He has no idea, does he?”

With a mental shake of the head, Grace acknowledged her question. “He has no idea about what?”

“Elliot doesn’t know you’ve fallen in love with him.”

Even if she wanted to answer, she couldn’t. Her throat felt tight and swollen while her heart thumped wildly in her chest.

“Don’t worry,” Evelyn whispered. “I won’t tell anyone. Your secret is safe.”

“There’s nothing to tell,” Grace replied, trying to regain her equilibrium. Their passion for each other helped them to forget the past that’s all. “I like him a great deal. But we’re different people, from different worlds. I could never be happy here.”

“Where could you be happy?”

Elliot’s bed was the first place that sprung to mind. A few days ago such a thought would have terrified her. After finding someone who worshipped her mind and body, would she ever be able to settle for a solitary life in Cobham?

“I have no idea anymore,” she replied honestly. “I like gazing out over fields and hills. I like breathing fresh air, running while the wind blows my hair. I enjoy reading and quiet walks through the forest."

"Elliot has an estate in Yorkshire."

Grace gave a weak smile. "I would never ask him to leave London. Besides, he has his friend Leo to think of, and I believe he would soon grow tired of looking at the same face each day."

It felt better to be honest with Evelyn and with herself. Had it not been for Caroline disappearing off into the night, she would have never met Elliot Markham.

A smile touched her lips.

Despite the bleak circumstances, she would never regret the time she'd spent with him. Her attraction to him was like a bittersweet addiction. It felt painful at times. Yet she longed to be near him, dreamed of his touch. With him, she felt wild and reckless. Without him, she wondered if she'd shrink back into the woman who shied away from intimacy, who bent to the will of others far too easily.

"We shall see," Evelyn replied with a smug look on her face.

While contemplating Evelyn's comment, she glanced around the room. "Am I imagining it, or do people keep staring at us?"

"No, you're not imagining it. I suspect they're curious about the likeness between you and Caroline. Come, let's stroll around and see who accidentally bumps into us to force an introduction."

As they moved around the perimeter of the dance floor, Grace grew more aware of the whispers and sly glances.

"There's Leo," Evelyn said as she stared at a gentleman surrounded by a group of ladies giggling and playing with their fans. She waited for him to glance in their direction.

He appeared vastly different when not dressed in his vibrant and slightly comical costume. Despite looking older, more masculine, he still held a boyish charm which his female admirers seemed to find vastly appealing. Grace wondered how they would perceive him if they witnessed his sharp teeth and black eyes.

Dragging himself away from the group, he sauntered over to them. "Evelyn," he said, bowing gracefully over her hand. "And Mrs. Denton. How nice to see you again."

"Have you had any luck extracting information from that gaggle of gossiping geese?" Evelyn said with a chuckle.

Leo nodded. "All I had to do was mention Mrs. Denton's likeness to her sister and they couldn't wait to enlighten me as to the state of current events."

Grace couldn't hide her impatience. "What did they say? Do they know anything?"

"Oh, they think they know everything."

Evelyn touched her arm. "Remember, we must try to extract the truth from a whole host of vicious lies. Prepare yourself as it may be rather unpleasant."

"Let us walk out onto the terrace," Leo said. He nodded to the open doors and then followed them outside. "It's a bit breezy, but we won't stay out here too long."

"Well?" Grace asked, turning to face him once noting they were alone. "Do not keep any of it from me. Tell me the worst."

"No one seemed to notice Caroline has not been about for a few days. When I mentioned it, someone said she'd probably gone abroad with a lover. Someone said she needs to hide from her creditors. Another said she probably has"—he stopped and cleared his throat—"said she has syphilis."

Grace gulped. "They are all lies. Every single one of them. Who plans to go abroad and not take a single item with them?"

"I agree with Grace," Evelyn said. "None of it rings true."

Leo brushed his hand through his hair. His warm brown eyes held a hint of compassion. "Elliot asked me to speak to Lady Sudley, but apparently she is ill. Only Lord Sudley is in attendance this evening."

"Are you gossiping about me now, Leo?"

Grace would recognise Elliot's voice anywhere. She looked beyond Leo's shoulder as Elliot and Alexander came to join them.

"Your lemonade." His tone sounded rich and languid as he handed her the glass. He looked so dangerously exquisite in his black coat. Hearing what others thought of Caroline had affected her mood and she wished they were alone so he could help her forget. Noticing the change in her, he narrowed his gaze. "Is everything all right?"

"We were discussing what I'd heard about Caroline Rosemond," Leo said. "I think we have established it is all lies. The only other conversation I was party to relates to her relationship with Mr. Henshaw."

Elliot straightened. "Lord Henshaw's son?"

Leo nodded. "The youngest one, Mark."

"Mark?" Grace gasped. It was the first credible piece of information they'd had. "Where does he live?"

All three gentlemen looked at her blankly.

"Wherever he lives," Leo began, "you won't find him there now. He's gone off on a *Grand Tour*." He shuffled uncomfortably on the spot. "Are you certain your sister didn't decide to follow him and in all the excitement simply neglected to tell you?"

Doubt flared.

"Caroline wouldn't do that to me." Grace's tone lacked the conviction her words implied. Caroline had always been flighty and self-absorbed.

Leo held his hands up in surrender. "I'm just saying, perhaps she was in love with him. Love has been the cause of many a selfish and scandalous act."

If Caroline was with child, perhaps Mr. Henshaw was the gentleman responsible for her condition. In those circumstances, she could imagine her sister acting thoughtlessly, desperately.

"Well, we can hardly knock on Lord Henshaw's door and ask him," Alexander offered. "Who else would know?"

Elliot's eyes grew wide, and he sucked in a breath. "It has just dawned on me. Mr. Henshaw has a sister. Lady Sudley is just a year older."

"I knew it," Grace cried, feeling somewhat smug and was tempted to punch the air in triumph. "The lady knows far more than she led me to believe. But we can't ask her about it now as she's not here."

"You said Lord Sudley is here," Evelyn said. "He may know something. At the very least I'm sure he knows where his wife's brother lives."

Leo sighed. "I thought we had already established Mr. Henshaw is not at home and has gone abroad."

"Yes, but perhaps one of his servants knows something," Evelyn said with frustration. "The question is which one of us will approach him?"

All heads turned to face Leo.

"Why me?" His hand flew to his chest as he took a step back. "I've done more than my fair share already. If it weren't for me, you'd all be none the wiser."

Elliot offered an arrogant smile. "Exactly. You've done marvellously up until now. No one will suspect you have any other motive other than enjoying the gossip."

Leo shook his head, but a smile played at the corners of his mouth. "If it were anyone else asking I'd tell them to go to the devil. I'll speak to Lord Sudley, but that's it. If I'm not careful, all the willing ladies will be taken and my evening will be utterly ruined. Then I'll have to spend the night trapped in the corner while the matrons reel off a list of the latest debutantes' accomplishments." He gave a small chuckle. "Do you know they spend hours perfecting getting in and out of a carriage? Apparently, one must alight in a modest and genteel manner if one has any hope of capturing a husband."

Alexander laughed. "Perhaps someone should tell them there are much better things to do in a carriage that boasts a much greater success of seeing them quickly wed."

"We are straying from the topic," Elliot interjected, pulling out his watch. "Let us part ways and reconvene on the terrace in thirty minutes. That should give Leo enough time to converse with Lord Sudley."

Alexander groaned as he looked down at Evelyn. "Please tell me I do not need to speak to anyone."

She smiled back at him. "We'll wander around, and you can see if you can hear anything of interest."

With Leo offering a curt nod, the trio walked back into the ballroom, leaving Grace and Elliot alone on the terrace.

Grace stepped closer to him as the air around them sparked to life. "I'm amazed Leo was able to learn so much and in such a short space of time. He does have one of those warm, approachable faces that would encourage the most hardened criminal to confess his sins."

Elliot glanced over his shoulder and then ran the backs of his fingers over her cheek, the strokes soft and tender. Desire flashed in his eyes or perhaps they simply acted as a mirror to her own.

"Leo can read a person's thoughts. He can sense things others cannot. We all can. It is a symptom of our affliction. He picks up threads of feelings and knows how to respond."

They could all read a person's innermost thoughts? Surely not.

She could feel her heart racing as an obvious question sprung to mind. "Did you … can you read my thoughts?"

Instantly, she tried to clear her mind. To think of nothing was far more difficult than she imagined. She tried to banish all foolish notions of love and of living with him in Yorkshire. But she couldn't shake the bone-deep need for him. She couldn't stop the memories forming, of him buried inside her or the ecstasy she felt when her release pulsed through her.

"Can you?" she repeated, trying to keep the panic from her voice.

"Sometimes. When my mind is calm. When your thoughts are more coherent. The more powerful the thought, the easier it is to read."

Judging by the sinful way his gaze wandered over her hair and mouth, she knew he was listening to her now. Terrified her mind would betray her and reveal a deep affection for him, she found her only hope was to focus on her physical need.

I want you, Elliot.

The thought barged past all others in its fight for supremacy, obliterating her fears for Caroline as it struggled for prominence. This infatuation she had for him overpowered all else.

Guilt was a potent emotion, too. Perhaps she should be mingling and dancing instead of fawning over her lover.

"No one will tell you anything," he suddenly said. "You're here tonight to serve as a reminder, as bait for the wagging tongues. Leo will discover Henshaw's address. He is extremely persuasive. And when we leave here, we will go there directly."

Grace stared at him.

"I feel your guilt," he continued by way of an explanation. "But there is no more you can do. I feel your passion, too, Grace. I feel it burning so brightly within you I can't focus on anything else. My head feels dizzy, filled with the need to sate our desires."

Oh, she wanted him so desperately.

Every step closer to Caroline took her a step further away from him.

Was it wrong of her to act so selfishly?

Was it wrong of her to let others do her bidding so she could relish in the feel of her lover's warm embrace? Never had she put her own needs before the needs of her friends and family.

"Come," he said, taking her hand, placing it in the crook of his arm and leading her back into the ballroom. "Perhaps it is the scoundrel in me. Perhaps I am guilty of being selfish and unfeeling. But I need to have you all to myself."

"Where will we go?" She offered no protest. How could she when every fibre of her being was addicted to his taste and his touch? A beautiful madness consumed her. She wanted nothing more than to be carried away to a place where all her wants and desires could come to fruition.

"Any place where we can be alone." There was a sense of urgency in his voice. He needed her, too, and all her worries were blown away like loose leaves in the wind.

As they made their way through the crowd, he led her out through a door to a narrow hallway. There were a few people milling about, and so they stopped, conversed, pretended to admire a painting.

I need you now, Grace.

The words echoed through her mind, and she shot round to face him. "I heard you. I heard your thought."

"I wondered if you might."

She could feel the raw masculine power emanating from him. The intoxicating energy infused her being. "What does that mean?"

He glanced over her shoulder, stepped back into the alcove and tried the door to find it open. "I'll show you what it means," he said as he pulled her inside.

CHAPTER 16

The heavy thrum of desire beat its potent rhythm, hard and powerful. Elliot could no longer control his actions. As soon as the door reconnected with the jamb, he pulled Grace into an embrace, pushing her back against the wooden panel and claiming her mouth.

She threw her gloves to the floor, ran her hot palms up over his chest and clutched his shoulders. Frantic hands raced over his back, her bare fingers creeping up to run through his hair as his tongue thrust wildly against hers.

Grace arched her back and pressed her willing body into his.

The sensual movement caused Elliot to moan into her mouth.

The need to mate with her was the most intense feeling he had ever experienced. It went beyond a physical need.

There were no words to define it.

Her sweet taste fed his craving. The smell of her hair and skin flooded his senses to calm and excite at the same time.

While the guests in the packed ballroom were busy drinking and dancing, he imagined positioning himself between her cushioned thighs and pushing inside her core. The strokes would be long and slow and deep. Possessive. The moist sound coupled with her little pants and groans would be music to his ears. Her body would sing to his tune, the beautiful aria drifting out to express her pleasure, her appreciation.

Always for him.

Only for him.

As he tore his lips away in his eagerness to lock the door, he peered out into the dim room. The harp's shiny gilt frame caught his attention; the pianoforte took centre stage to the rows of chairs lined up ready for the recital.

At any moment, there could be a knock on the door. The elderly matrons eagerly forming a queue outside would be keen to enter, keen to find a seat near the front. Their reproachful gazes would drift over Grace's mussed hair, over the shabby state of her clothing. The unmistakable scent of sated lust in the air would confirm their suspicions.

No one would give him a second glance.

In everyone's eyes, Grace would become the errant knight's cape: something relegated to the muddy gutter. Something to trample over. Something beneath them.

"We can't stay here," he suddenly said, though his throbbing erection jerked in protest. "We'll be discovered."

"Why?" She glanced around the room. The glassy lustre of desire faded from her eyes as she became aware of her surroundings. "Is there to be a concert tonight?"

He shrugged. "I don't know. But I will not take the chance. I'll not expose you to the degrading taunts and snide comments if we're caught."

It hit him then. With every other woman, every other time, he'd not given a damn about the repercussions.

But he cared now.

He cared deeply.

Elliot sucked in a breath as he let the thought seep into his consciousness.

Grace smoothed her hands down the front of her gown, drawing his gaze to her full, sumptuous breasts waiting to be released from their silk prison, waiting for the feel of his fingers, for the flick of his tongue.

Bloody hell.

He'd never felt so frustrated. But the need to protect her outweighed the raging of his rampant loins.

"You're worried we will be discovered alone together?" Grace placed her hand on his arm. "Elliot, I'm sure those who have seen us together have already made certain assumptions."

Elliot rubbed the back of his neck. "It is not the same as stumbling upon us half dressed. Whether you're a widow or not, it is hardly discreet."

She smiled and a strange sensation filled his chest. "You still haven't told me," she said softly. "You haven't told me why I heard your thoughts."

For a moment he wished he were mute. To reveal the truth would mean admitting to a feeling he had run and hid from for years. He didn't want to care about anyone and the thought of saying the words aloud scared the hell out of him. Partly because he refused to be a foolish dreamer. Partly because he feared disappointment. Happiness always came at a price.

He sighed. "It's because a connection exists between us." Indeed, he feared their attraction had grown into something else. Something deeper, more profound. "Our joining has brought a heightened level of awareness. That is why you can hear me."

"Will it always be the case?"

Elliot knew what she was asking. When they parted company, would the connection always exist? When consumed with sadness or grief, would he feel it, too? Would he know when she felt love in her heart for another? Would he know when she felt desire for her new beau—when her body shook from the effects of her release?

"Honestly, I do not know," he answered, fearing such a thing was possible.

"You have never experienced it before?" she asked. "You have never made a connection with another?"

"No." He swallowed deeply, not wanting to admit he was struggling to navigate this uncharted territory. Nor did he want to admit he had witnessed the same thing occur with Alexander and Evelyn. "Other than Alexander and Leo, no one has ever heard my thoughts."

"Oh."

"This is all new to me." He waved his hand back and forth between them. "Whatever exists between us is hard to define."

She gave a knowing smile. "It is all new to me, too, Elliot."

The air between them buzzed. The sensitive skin on his lips tingled. His chest felt warm, tight. As the throbbing ache between his legs pulsed, he knew they had to leave for he was too weak to fight his need for her.

"It must be time to leave," he said, avoidance being the only way to suppress his desire. "They'll be waiting for us on the terrace."

"Well, we should not keep them waiting," she said with a heavy sigh. "There'll be time to talk later."

If he had his way, there would be time to do more than talk.

The sound of laughter resonating along the hallway captured his attention. Panic flared. Elliot put his ear to the door. As the sound dissipated, he prised the door from the jamb and peered outside.

"Quick, the hallway is empty. We must go now."

He took her hand as they hurried from the room, placing it in the crook of his arm as they attempted to walk calmly and casually back into the ballroom.

Alexander and Evelyn were already waiting outside on the terrace. They were standing but a hair's breadth apart. Alexander brushed a stray tendril from Evelyn's face, his knuckles stroking her cheek as she gazed longingly into his eyes.

Elliot's reaction to the intimate exchange shocked him.

Jealousy delivered a sharp stab to his chest.

Guilt followed with a blow to his stomach.

The beautiful, passionate lady at his side had been thrust into a dark room to be ravaged in secret by a seasoned seducer, offering nothing more than the use of his body. Other couples openly demonstrated the love, respect and admiration they shared.

"There you are." Evelyn turned to face them, her gaze drifting down to Grace's hands before offering a smirk. "You appear to have mislaid something."

Grace gasped. "My gloves. I must have left them in the music room."

"I'll go back," Elliot said.

"Nonsense. I'll go. I'll only be a minute. While I'm gone, perhaps you should go in search of Leo."

Alexander snorted. "No doubt he has been waylaid by some lady or other. He's probably forgotten all about the task we set him."

"What if he's failed to discover what we need to know?" There was no mistaking the panic in Grace's voice.

"Don't worry." Elliot turned to face her. "If need be, I'll speak to Lord Sudley, and I'll not leave here until I do."

Grace hurried to the music room, sneaking back inside when she thought no one was looking. She spotted her gloves on the floor behind the door and breathed a sigh of relief. It would not take much for someone to find them and realise she was the only lady at the ball with bare hands.

Not that it mattered.

Hopefully, this would be the last time she'd need to go out in Society.

As she bent down to retrieve them, she noticed the light in the room diminish, heard the door creak. When she straightened, she almost expired on the spot and had to put her hand to her heart to stop it bursting from her chest.

"Lord Barrington." She gasped as the gentleman closed the door firmly behind him.

It occurred to her to scream. Surely he would behave himself in such a crowded place. But the room wasn't crowded; it was empty, dark, and they were alone.

"Forgive me for barging in here unannounced," he said, waving his hands in the air. "I have recently been made aware that you are not, in fact, Miss Rosemond. I know I acted appallingly the other night. Indeed, I still bear the scars. Punishment for my uncouth behaviour, though I only have a vague recollection of events."

Grace noticed the shadow of a bruise on his cheek, the way he stood slightly off balance favouring his right side. While she appreciated the apology, something about the gentleman's manner unsettled her.

"Well, you were not to know," she said, desperate to flee the room and be reunited with Elliot on the terrace. "But you cannot behave in such a disrespectful manner. I do not think Caroline would appreciate your high-handed approach."

She should not have made her feelings known.

Not because her opinion lacked merit, but because the gentleman had a strange look in his eye. A flicker of disdain. A dislike for women who spoke their mind.

"You are so like her in many ways." He stared at the mole on her cheek before his gaze moved to her lips. "Indeed, a gentleman might convince himself you were one and the same."

A bolt of fear shot through her, and she glanced at the closed door. "But you know that is not the case. You know we are kin. We are sisters. You know I am not Caroline."

He shrugged. "What does it matter? You look the same." His beady black eyes fell to the neckline of her gown. "And you appear to have an advantage over your sister. Still, you behave in the same free and easy manner. Else why would you rush into a dark room to reclaim your gloves? Once Markham has taken what he wants, he will discard you without thought or care."

"You make it sound as though I am a pawn in a game. I am not ignorant to the tactics employed by men. But I am bound to no one."

Lord Barrington took a step closer. Grace shuffled two steps back.

"But you could be. I shall make you the same proposition I made Caroline." Like a man suffering from a serious lack of sustenance, his hungry gaze devoured her. "Indeed, I may be inclined to increase my original offer as I fear I shall be getting rather more for my money."

It took a tremendous amount of effort not to slap him.

"And what did you offer?" Grace took another step back. The aisle between the rows of chairs was the only means of escape. She would have no option but to barge past Lord Barrington's large frame.

Lord Barrington gave a sly grin. "A house, fully staffed and equipped, which I will maintain for as long as you maintain me."

Repulsed by his comment, Grace shivered. Had he not accosted her when he believed her to be Caroline, Lord Barrington would be the prime suspect on her list of gentlemen capable of doing serious harm to a lady.

"Of course, there would be a substantial monthly income," he continued with an indolent wave. "The use of a carriage and an account at a modiste of your choosing."

"So, essentially you are asking me to be your mistress?" Grace's only thought was to keep the man talking in the hope of escaping. Her options were limited. She could attempt to run past him. She could climb across the chairs or pick one up and hit him.

Then another option struck her. Elliot had said he could feel her passion. He had said their connection made it possible to hear one another's thoughts.

Elliot. Come quickly.

She poured every ounce of affection she had for him into the silent plea.

"Yes, I suppose *mistress* is the appropriate term. But I prefer to think of it as a form of friendship where we barter and exchange services. A mutually satisfying arrangement."

Mutually satisfying? The man was delusional.

Grace raised her chin to stave off her anxiety. "And what exactly would you require in return?"

Elliot. Hurry. I need you.

"I think you know," Barrington said with a chuckle and her stomach churned at the thought.

"I … I shall need time to consider your proposal."

Barrington's expression darkened, and he clenched his jaw. "You will bloody well tell me now. I have spent weeks chasing after your sister, and I'll be damned if I'll do the same again."

The cold blade of fear traced a line down her back. "And if my answer is no?"

The gentleman's face twisted into an ugly scowl as he stepped forward. Grace found she couldn't take another step without the edge of the pianoforte digging into her back.

"Then you will leave me no choice" came the frustrated reply. "I shall have to persuade you."

It was now or never, Grace thought.

The man held his elbow awkwardly against his ribs. Gathering every ounce of courage she had, she darted towards his weakest side.

Initially, the shock caused Barrington to stumble. But he was a large man with long strides and like that first fateful night, he caught her with ease.

"God damn you. Why will you not yield?" Barrington dragged her back to face him, his pincer-like grip digging into her upper arm. "Would you rather be used by the likes of Markham and his ilk? I'm offering you a home and money. You never need worry again."

"You have lost your mind if you believe I would spend another moment in your company. You disgust me."

"Do not forget your place, girl." A drop of saliva hit her cheek. "You'll speak to me with more respect."

"Get your rotten hands off me." She tried to keep calm, but images of Henry flooded her vision. Lord Barrington appeared similar in many ways: his height, his breadth, the stench of stale tobacco lingering on his clothes. His breath smelt sickly sweet from drinking copious amounts of brandy.

Part of her wanted to sag to the floor in surrender—just as she had always done. Part of her wanted to punch and kick him for every horrid, unbearable moment she had been forced to endure.

When Barrington lowered his head and attempted to claim her mouth, she kicked him in the shin. The flimsy slipper barely made contact, and he cried out in anger as opposed to pain.

"Why, you little whore. I should whip you where you stand."

A deep growl permeated the air, the sound threatening, possessive.

As her gaze flew to Barrington's horrified face, she knew Elliot was standing behind her. She closed her eyes in silent prayer.

"Let her go, Barrington." Elliot's tone sounded calm, measured. Yet she could feel his rage pulse through her. "Step away. Else there'll be hell to pay."

Barrington released her arm and made the mistake of stepping back. Elliot flew past her in an instant and from the look of sheer terror on Barrington's face, Grace knew Elliot's eyes were coal black, that the sharp points of his teeth overhung his bottom lip.

"Leave me alone … stay away I say," Barrington spluttered as he stumbled over his own feet, grabbing on to the empty chairs to steady his balance. "What sort of m-monster are you?"

"One capable of ripping your throat from your measly body." Elliot kicked at the wooden chair legs sending them scattering as he drove his quarry further back. "One who'll make you pay for your lecherous ways."

Barrington held his hands up to shield his face as he came to an abrupt halt in front of the pianoforte. "What … what are you going to do to me?"

Grace could not see the expression on Elliot's face, but she heard him snarl. The sound was vicious, unforgiving.

"Elliot. Wait." Grace almost choked in her eagerness to get the words out. "You've frightened him enough."

Elliot grabbed the lapels of Barrington's coat. "I don't trust him. What if I'm not here to protect you next time?"

A commotion erupted behind them as Leo, Alexander and Evelyn burst in through the door.

"Hell and damnation," Alexander growled as Elliot glanced over his shoulder. "We cannot let anyone in here. We cannot let anyone see him like this."

Just a glimpse of Elliot's countenance confirmed what she suspected; the beast inside was primed and ready for attack.

Leo put his hand on Alexander's arm. "Take Evelyn outside. Block the door and don't let anyone in. Be persuasive if you have to."

"Get him the hell off me." Barrington's voice conveyed his fear.

"I don't give a damn what he does to you, Barrington," Leo said, marching towards them as Alexander and Evelyn slipped outside. "But I do give a damn what happens to him."

Grace's heart thumped so hard she could feel it in her throat. In truth, she wanted Elliot to hurt Lord Barrington. To teach him a lesson. She wanted to punish the lord for hounding her sister, for being a self-absorbed prig, for reminding her of Henry.

But another feeling overpowered all others.

Hurting Barrington would only bring Elliot more pain, more regrets, more memories to bury behind a false facade.

Grace rushed forward, touching Leo on the arm. "Let me try. Just give me one chance. Please."

Leo's gaze searched her face, and he sighed. "One chance. But hurry."

She came to stand beside Elliot.

"Can't you bring your dog to heel?" Barrington scoffed, finding an ounce of courage. But Elliot flexed his jaw causing the man to whimper.

"Be quiet." Grace turned to Elliot. "Let him go, Elliot. You're the one who's always so calm, so in control. I need you to be calm now. I need you to listen to me."

"He needs to pay for what he's done." When Elliot's gaze met hers, she sucked in a breath. Yet while his countenance conveyed the horror of his affliction, she saw a hint of sorrow in his black eyes. "I need to know he can never hurt you again."

A well of emotion erupted inside.

Barrington writhed as he tried to shake himself free. Despite being smaller and leaner in frame, Elliot seemed to have the strength of ten men, and he tightened his grip on his prey.

Grace cupped Elliot's cheek, and he turned to look at her. "If you hurt him, you will only be hurting yourself. I won't let that happen." She swallowed deeply, stood on the tips of her toes and placed a soft, chaste kiss on his terrifying teeth. "I love you."

Her throat felt tight as tears welled and threatened to fall. As he stared into her eyes, flickers of green invaded the darkness. The red veins dissipated, retreated, surrendered to the light.

Relief coursed through her.

It didn't matter that she had bared her soul to him. Vulnerability was a feeling she had dealt with many times before.

"I love you," she repeated, determined that no matter what happened between them he would never forget her words. He would always know someone loved him for who he was, regardless of his affliction.

Leo stepped forward and covered Elliot's hands. "Let me deal with Barrington. He'll remember none of this. I'll convince him to change his ways so you never need worry."

Elliot let go of Barrington's coat and the man sagged against the pianoforte.

"You will stay where you are." Leo's command carried a

certain power, a gravity that could not be denied or disobeyed. "There is much to discuss, Lord Barrington."

Grace took Elliot's hand and led him to the opposite end of the room. While he remained quiet, a little subdued, the look of longing in his eyes was all she needed to bring her comfort.

"I have the information we need," Leo called back over his shoulder. "If you feel able, we could make a call tonight."

Grace turned to Elliot. "If you want to go home, I can go with Leo. I'll come and—"

"I'm going with you," he said, his tone somewhat solemn. "I'll not leave you. Not until I know you've got the answers you need. Not until I know you're happy and back home safely in Cobham."

Back home in Cobham?

She tried to listen to his thoughts. She tried to feel the emotion she could hear infused within his words. Confusion was the only thing she felt. Did he really want to send her back to Cobham? Was there no part of him that wanted her to stay?

Once she had discovered the mystery surrounding Caroline's disappearance, her work would be far from over. Unravelling the mystery of Elliot Markham's complex emotions would be a far greater task.

CHAPTER 17

With his carriage still stationary, Elliot lounged back in the seat, his intense gaze focused on the lady sitting opposite him. Grace looked up from her lap, her weak smiling revealing her apprehension.

He had been ready to end Barrington's life.

In the same way Alexander had been ready to end Mr. Sutherby's at Mytton Grange.

But what did it mean?

"You're sure you want to go tonight?" Evelyn asked, breaking the heavy silence. She sat next to Grace, leaving a space at the end for Leo—when he finally arrived. "I'm assuming Mr. Henshaw's house is somewhere in London."

"I suppose we will know more when Leo joins us." Alexander shuffled in the seat next to him, his impatience evident in his tone. "How long does it take to rid a man of his memory?"

"No doubt some woman has delayed his departure." Elliot was in need of a distraction. Prolonging the conversation forced him to abandon all memories of Grace's amorous declarations. "We'll know the answer if the air suddenly becomes choked with the smell of cheap perfume."

"It will be a wasted journey. It's unlikely we'll find anything of interest there." Alexander threw his hands up when Evelyn flashed him an irate glare. "What? I am just being honest."

"Lord Hale is right," Grace said with a sigh. "I'm sure there'll be no one home, and it will all have been a complete waste of time."

Elliot was determined to find some useful piece of information this evening. His emotions felt like the over-tightened strings of a viola. One more small incident and he would most likely snap. "Whether there's anyone home or not, I shall insist on searching the property."

Alexander snorted. "Well, if you smash the window don't think you're using my coat to muffle the sound. Not after the last time. I itch every time I wear it yet still can't find the source of my irritation."

"I have discovered a new technique." Elliot couldn't help but grin as he imagined the scenario. "This time, I'll just need to borrow your hat."

Before Alexander could protest, the door flew open, and Leo climbed inside. He settled down next to Evelyn and, despite appearing a little breathless, there were no telltale signs to suggest the reason for his delay.

"I swear I have never met a man as stubborn as Lord Barrington." Leo exhaled loudly. "He is so obsessed with securing a mistress it took an age to persuade him otherwise. I was beginning to think I had lost my touch."

Elliot sat forward. "You are certain there will be no more trouble from him?"

"Yes. I've convinced him he needs a wife and sent him off in the direction of the wallflowers." Leo's playful expression turned to one of concern as he focused his attention on Elliot. "Are you fully recovered from your ordeal? I must say it is the first time I have ever seen you lose control like that. Normally, I'm the one raging from the rooftops."

Was he fully recovered?

Never in his life had he felt so close to murdering another. Hot molten rage had coursed through his veins until all he could do was unleash the Devil's own fury. It hadn't subsided completely. He still wanted to wring Barrington's neck. But he had recovered sufficiently to proceed with the night's planned event.

"I did not lose control," Elliot corrected. He had always been the one to offer advice, always the voice of reason. Though in truth, he scarcely knew what to think anymore. When Grace had placed a tender kiss on his hideous features, all logical thought abandoned him. "Barrington deserved to be taught a lesson, and I was happy to oblige."

Leo cast him a smug grin. "If you say so, although I'm relieved Mrs. Denton knew how to calm your volatile spirit."

I love you.

Grace's words invaded his thoughts—obliterating his barricade to demand his surrender.

Had she made the declaration just to calm him?

Was it simply her intention to cause a distraction?

"You said you knew where Mr. Henshaw resided," Elliot said to steer Leo away from revealing what he had heard. "Jump out and relay the instructions to Gibbs."

Leo gave a polite nod. "I've already told him. He's just waiting for your signal to depart."

Elliot thumped the carriage roof and braced himself as it lurched forward.

"Well?" Alexander said as the conveyance settled into a steadier pace.

"Well, what?" Leo shrugged.

The force from Alexander's exasperated sigh could have blown out fifty candles. "Where does this Mr. Henshaw live?"

"Oh. He lives on Hanover Street. Lord Sudley took little persuading to reveal the information though I suspect he's still wandering the ballroom somewhat dazed."

Alexander folded his arms across his chest. "And what will we do when we get there?"

All heads turned to face Elliot.

"First, we must observe the property," Elliot replied. "Enter by whatever means necessary. Search until we find something to lead us to Caroline Rosemond's whereabouts."

Grace cleared her throat. "Then I pray we are successful, my lord." She turned her attention to the other occupants. "You have all done more than I could ever have hoped. Indeed, after tonight, I shall ask no more of you. Whether our search proves successful or not, I must consider returning home to Cobham without her, without ever knowing what has happened."

The gravity of her words hit him like a vicious blow to the stomach. The force robbed him of his breath, and he resisted the need to gasp.

In Cobham, she would be safe. She would be far away from the malicious tongues determined to cause her pain. She would not be such an easy target for every scoundrel looking to tup a courtesan.

An image of her wandering the idyllic countryside flooded his vision. He saw her clutching the arm of some other gentleman as they navigated the muddy lane, laughing as they dodged the rain when caught in an unexpected shower. He saw her face alight with pleasure as the fictitious beau smothered her in kisses. He saw the look of adoration in her eyes when she held her child in her arms for the first time.

The pain grew more intense, like a blunt blade twisting in his gut.

"Then let us hope the night proves fruitful," Evelyn said, and he had to grit his teeth for fear of throwing them all out onto the pavement, riding off with Grace as his prisoner and never letting her go.

Leo wiped the window with his glove. "We're here. I instructed Gibbs to pull up on the opposite side of the street. It's that one." He pointed to a townhouse in the middle of the terrace.

They all leant forward, almost bumping heads in their eagerness to observe the building.

"The house looks cold and empty," Alexander said. "I see no light, no sign anyone's home."

"What of Henshaw's staff?" Elliot asked.

Leo shrugged. "I assume they've either been deployed elsewhere, or they're still tending to the property in Henshaw's absence."

"Well, there is only one way to find out." Elliot tugged at the lapels of his coat and the ends of his sleeves. "I'll simply knock the door and persuade whoever answers to let me in."

"Perhaps I should come with you," Grace said. "It is my fault we're all here."

"It's not your fault, Grace." Elliot gave her a reassuring smile as he edged forward. "And it damn well better not be Caroline's fault, either."

"Wait!" Alexander put his arm out to stop him from moving. "Someone is leaving."

Grace shuffled forward and gasped. "Is that … is that Lady Sudley? I thought she was supposed to be ill."

"It is Lady Sudley," Elliot confirmed as he watched the lady scurry down the street, glancing nervously over her shoulder as she headed towards Hanover Square. "But why is she out on her own, walking the streets at this time of night?"

Leo turned to face him. "As she only lives in the square, I assume she did not want to trouble her coachman."

It was Evelyn's turn to gasp. "I've just realised something. In Caroline's diary, perhaps it wasn't Markham. The letters M and N look so similar and are often mistaken."

Logic told him Evelyn's theory was correct. "You mean she met with Mark in Hanover Street."

"Precisely."

Grace cleared her throat. "If Caroline was meeting him here, then she could have left to go abroad with Mr. Henshaw. She could be touring the Continent while I've been darting about like a March hare."

If that were true, Caroline Rosemond was as cold and as heartless as he imagined. God, he hoped there'd been a mistake, and some other explanation could be found.

"Right," he said with an element of determination. "I'm going inside. Wait here until I give a signal to follow."

"I'm coming with you." Grace grabbed his arm and their gazes locked.

How could he refuse her anything when she looked at him with such sorrow in her eyes? All he could think of was seeing her happy and untroubled. "Very well. You may come," he said, dismissing the strange sense of foreboding writhing through his body.

Grace trotted along beside him, trying to keep up with his long strides. Did his eagerness stem from a desire to bring an end to her worries or a determination to send her back to Cobham?

If only he would give her a small clue, a tiny indication of his true feelings.

Mentally chastising herself for being far too absorbed with her own problems, Grace shook the thoughts from her mind, intent on focusing on the task at hand.

Elliot rapped on Henshaw's front door, and Grace shuffled a little to the left to widen the gap between them to a more respectable distance. Due to the intimacy they'd shared, she felt more at ease when she could feel his touch. Even if it was only the sleeve of his coat brushing against her cape.

How would she fare when they were separated by miles, not mere inches?

Failing to rouse a response, Elliot knocked again. After a brief silence, she heard the faint sound of shuffling feet.

"Sorry, my lady" came the woman's voice as the door creaked open. "I wasn't expecting you back so—"

The woman's gaze shot up from the floor, and she jerked her head back as though reeling from an invisible punch.

"Mrs. Jones?" Grace narrowed her gaze as her mind attempted to confirm what her eyes were seeing. The presence of Caroline's servant caused a mixture of relief and curiosity to course through her. "What are you doing here?"

"You know this woman?" Elliot asked in a sombre tone.

"Mrs. Denton, I … I thought …" Mrs. Jones shuffled on the spot. Her chubby lips moved up and down rapidly, but no words escaped.

Grace turned to Elliot. "Mrs. Jones is Caroline's cook. The one I've not seen for days."

"I c-can explain," she stuttered.

"Stand aside," Elliot commanded, his tone stern, unyielding. "You will let us in."

Mrs. Jones struggled to obey, but Elliot put his hand on the door to open it fully. "Perhaps I did not make myself clear. You will let us in."

The woman nodded as she stepped back to usher them inside.

"Is Mr. Henshaw at home?" Elliot did not look at the woman but glanced at the doors off the hallway.

"He … he's away. Gone abroad. I'm … I'm keeping house during his absence."

"Where are the servants?" he said, opening the first door and peering inside.

"Norfolk. They've gone to Lord Henshaw's house near Hunstanton."

"Why?" he demanded.

"The tapestries needed cleaning. There's dust everywhere since they've had the roof fixed. My lady sent them to help, thought they would like the opportunity to take some country air."

Grace could not contain herself and blurted, "Have you seen Caroline? Is she here?"

Elliot swung around and stared at Mrs. Jones.

The woman's gaze darted everywhere except at them. "Yes. Yes, I've seen her. There's no need for concern."

"She's here," Elliot cried, racing to the stairs and climbing them two at a time. "Caroline is here."

Grace followed him while Mrs. Jones plodded behind shouting, "Wait. You can't go up there. Wait. It's not what you think."

Elliot stopped on the landing and scanned the closed doors.

"What is it?" Grace struggled to suppress her anxiety. "You're certain she's here?"

He nodded as he gazed up at the ceiling. "Up here," he said, charging up the next flight to the upper floor.

They moved along the landing, trying doors and peering inside. Only one door was locked.

Mrs. Jones joined them on the upper floor, the effort taken to climb the stairs robbing her of breath. "She … she's fine," Mrs. Jones gasped. "She's just resting that's all."

"Open it." Elliot stabbed his finger at the door while Grace held her breath.

Could they have finally found what they'd spent days searching for?

Could Caroline be just a few feet away?

"Open it," Elliot demanded. "Else I'll break down the door."

Mrs. Jones picked up her chatelaine and flicked through the keys. Elliot and Grace crowded around her as the lock clicked, barging into the room as soon as she opened the door.

A candle burnt low on a dresser in the far corner of the room. The figure of a woman could be clearly seen lying beneath the coverlet on the narrow bed.

Grace rushed forward, recognising her sister instantly despite her pale complexion. "Caroline. Caroline." She took her sister's hand in her own and tapped it gently. "Can you hear me?"

Elliot came to stand on the opposite side of the bed. He

studied Caroline's gaunt face, put his hand to her head, lifted her lids and examined her eyes.

"Is she asleep?" Grace asked.

"In a manner of speaking," he replied cryptically but then turned to Mrs. Jones. "Have you administered any medicine? A tincture or tonic?"

Mrs. Jones gave a curt nod. "Only a tincture of laudanum as my lady instructed."

"What are you administering it for?"

Mrs. Jones stepped further into the room. "When Miss Rosemond came here she tripped, fell and hurt her head. My lady sent for me. She was worried and thought it best I took care of her."

Grace gasped. "Why didn't you send for me? You left me alone, without so much as a word. I have been frantic with worry."

Mrs. Jones had the decency to look ashamed. "Lady Sudley said Miss Rosemond would be better in a day or two. She said it would be best to keep it quiet, so as not to cause any more trouble for my master."

"But Caroline has been here for almost a week," Grace countered.

Mrs. Jones shook her head. "Every day I have hoped she would be a bit better, so we could return home. But Lady Sudley said I must do what serves Mr. Henshaw best, what with me being in his employ. She said we must take care of Miss Rosemond in his absence. She said we must not move the patient until she's well."

"Something's amiss here," Elliot said, ignoring Mrs. Jones and coming to stand in front of her. "I suggest we take Caroline home in my carriage. That we remove her as quickly as possible. But ultimately the decision is yours."

Grace glanced at the lifeless body in the bed. Elliot was right. None of it made any sense. She saw no sign of a head injury though that didn't mean there wasn't one.

"I agree. I want to take her home. I'll call on a physician to come and examine her." Grace stepped closer, touched his arm, dismissing the warm feeling that raced through her body at the close contact. "We need to know if she's with child."

Elliot cupped her cheek, his thumb moving back and forth in tender strokes. Grace closed her eyes briefly, savouring the moment as she had no idea if she'd ever feel his touch again. "Trust me. She'll be right in no time. Come, we'll get help to move her."

"I'm afraid I can't let you do that."

The feminine voice sliced through the air. They turned to see Lady Sudley standing in the doorway, brandishing a pistol.

CHAPTER 18

"Lady Sudley. I'm pleased you could join us." Elliot said, failing to disguise the contempt in his tone. He despised weak women who chose weapons as a means to manipulate and control. Although Lady Sudley's hair was coal black, something about her arrogant countenance reminded him of the golden-haired devil in Bavaria.

"Step away from the bed." The lady waved the pistol back and forth between him and Grace, gesturing to the place where she wished them to stand. "I'm afraid now you've seen Miss Rosemond, I cannot let you leave."

"I don't understand. What's Caroline doing here?" Grace said, her tone revealing her distress. "And before you say anything more, I know it has nothing to do with a head injury."

"Well, no, you're right." Lady Sudley gave a sly grin. "It has nothing to do with an illness or an injury."

Mrs. Jones' hand flew to her chest. "But you said she had fallen. You said she couldn't be moved until she'd recovered and—"

"Oh, do be quiet, Mrs. Jones. I needed someone to care for her. Surely you don't expect me to cook her meals and empty her pot."

Elliot studied the exchange, trying to determine whether he could reach Lady Sudley before she fired the pistol. He would happily take a hit to the arm if it meant wiping the grin from her smug face.

But he would not endanger Grace.

If anything happened to her, he'd most likely rip the throats from everyone who crossed his path.

"I'm certain that when you've heard what I have to say, you will thank me," Lady Sudley said. "You will see this is the only feasible course of action."

"Does it have something to do with your brother?" Grace asked. "Has my sister wronged him in some way and now you're determined to seek your revenge?"

Lady Sudley laughed, the sound more an ear-piercing cackle. "If I sought revenge on all my brother's conquests, London would only be populated by men."

He noticed Lady Sudley's hand quiver. She could not hold the pistol straight for long. Her arm would grow heavier by the minute.

"If revenge is not the motivation, what is?" Elliot said as he edged forward.

Ignoring his question, she turned to Grace. "You have been married, Mrs. Denton. So Mrs. Jones tells me. Do you have children?"

Elliot observed Grace's expression with keen interest. The way she answered would reveal much, he thought. Would her words convey a deep sense of longing? Did she dream of raising a family? A dream he could never help her fulfil. Could she bear a life knowing she would never be a mother?

"No. I do not have children."

Her tone was blunt and concise.

She gave him nothing.

"I am so pleased to hear that. What sort of mother would you be, parading about town with your lover while your little treasures are tucked up in their beds wondering if you'll come home?"

Elliot had no idea where this conversation was heading, but he feared the lady possessed a distorted view of reality.

"I would be a very poor mother indeed," Grace replied, while Elliot used the distraction to shuffle forward.

"Do not come any closer, Lord Markham." Lady Sudley aimed the pistol directly at Grace's heart. "I will not hesitate. I will shoot."

Damn the woman.

He would have to use his powers of persuasion to get her to give up her weapon. Choosing the right time would be critical as she would become dazed, perhaps a little confused at first and he could not risk her firing at some imagined target.

"Some women do not deserve to experience such a precious gift," Lady Sudley continued, glancing at Caroline's still body in the bed. "Not while there are perfectly respectable ladies desperate to hold a babe in their arms. Ladies denied the opportunity at every turn."

Grace shrugged. "Nature has a way of deciding who or what best serves its purpose. There are many respectable ladies who would make appalling mothers. Just as there are street vendors whose exhaustive efforts to raise their children are to be commended."

Elliot glanced at Grace, admiration filling his chest. Her heart was kind, honest and good. She did not judge; she did not preach. She bore no preconceived notions or prejudices.

"I disagree." Lady Sudley stuck her nose in the air. "Respectability is everything. And so you can imagine my horror when Mark told me his whore would bear his child."

The whore she referred to was obviously Caroline Rosemond. Elliot touched Grace's hand as it hung by his side, an affectionate gesture to calm and soothe her spirit.

Grace exhaled loudly. "So it is true. Caroline is with child."

Lady Sudley snorted. "Why else would my brother flee the

country? He has never been one for responsibility. When I confronted him about his plans, he told me the apothecary dispensed medicine to help rid women of unwanted things. Can you believe he referred to his child as a *thing*?" She gave a satisfied grin before adding, "That's when I came up with my wonderful plan."

Elliot waved his hand over the scene. "If this is your wonderful plan, then you have made a series of miscalculations. Now, I believe it is time to put the pistol down and—"

"You do not understand." Lady Sudley's eyes widened. "I have already told my husband I am with child. He is delighted after fearing he had made a dreadful mistake in marrying me. What peer wants a barren wife?"

"I'm confused," Grace said. "Are you with child?"

Recognition dawned.

"No," Elliot said. "Lady Sudley plans to take Caroline's child and pass it off as her own. Am I right?"

"The child belongs to my brother, to my family. If he has no interest in it, then why shouldn't I? It solves all our problems. My brother will think the medicine worked. Miss Rosemond may continue her career as a courtesan without such a heavy burden, and I can give my husband the child he so desperately craves."

"You were going to keep Caroline here until the baby is born?" Grace asked incredulously.

"Of course not. I shall travel to my father's estate in Norfolk. It is far healthier for a child to be born in the country. Caroline will stay in a cottage, and when the time comes, I shall take the babe and return to London. You must see it is the best option all round."

Lady Sudley was deranged, a prime candidate for Bedlam.

Elliot could feel Grace's distress. "I assume Caroline does not agree with your wonderful plan?" he said.

"She will soon come round to the idea. I have money and will make her far too generous an offer to decline."

"And what of us?" Elliot asked as he focused on the lady's tired hand. Another minute and she would be forced to lower it completely. "No child wants a murderer for a mother. You said so yourself. Respectability is important."

"But surely you see the sense in my plan now?" Lady Sudley pleaded. "Surely you cannot oppose it?"

Grace turned to face him. "Perhaps Lady Sudley is right. Perhaps she would be a better mother to the child than Caroline."

Elliot searched her face. One look in her eyes told him what he needed to know. If they put the lady at ease, they had a better chance of taking the pistol.

However, the idea amounted to nothing more than a fleeting thought as a dull thud echoed through the hallway below.

"It's the door, my lady." Mrs. Jones hovered in the corner. "Should I go answer it?"

Lady Sudley raised the pistol and firmed her grip. "Ignore it. They will soon go away."

They all stood in silence as the persistent caller knocked again. No doubt Alexander and Leo sensed something was wrong and were keen to investigate. They would not walk away. Elliot conjured an image of Alexander demanding the use of Leo's coat to muffle the sound while he broke the window.

"Lower the pistol, Lady Sudley," Elliot said in as calm a voice as he could muster. "If you fire, you will certainly injure someone. Then I'm afraid your respectable neck will spend a few painful minutes wrestling with the hangman's noose."

"Can you not understand my dilemma?" she implored, focusing her attention on Grace. "Did you ever disappoint your husband? Do you know what it's like to spend every waking moment wondering how to make him happy?"

A sudden wave of sadness flooded Elliot's chest. He wanted to curse the lady for reminding Grace of Henry Denton's abusive ways.

"I understand perfectly," Grace said in a solemn, weary tone.

"It makes you feel inadequate, a failure. Every day you feel a little less whole. Nothing you do seems to make a difference and so you smile at the world and pretend you're happy. But inside you feel like a vine of thorns has wrapped itself around your heart, piercing it a thousand times over."

Elliot's heart ached, too, hearing her sad words.

He had never experienced another person's pain, not in the human sense. Indeed, it wasn't just a case of being aware of her feelings. The agony accompanying the memory felt real to him.

Lady Sudley appeared surprised at her response. "It is exactly like that."

Grace shook her head. "Then you must know, to control and abuse others to ease your sadness makes you just as guilty as your negligent husband. Do not become the monster you fear. You must tell him the truth."

Staring at a spot on the wooden floor, the lady considered Grace's words. "He'll despise me," she said, shaking her head and muttering to herself as she played out the conversation she would have with her husband.

"Put down the pistol, Lady Sudley," Elliot repeated.

He could sense the lady growing more agitated as she struggled to make a decision. Her gaze flitted back and forth between him and the bed. Her breathing sounded short and shallow.

The creak of a board outside the door caused Lady Sudley to swing around, and she jumped back in shock. Her hand jerked upwards just as the loud crack resonated through the room. Lady Sudley's shocked gasp was accompanied by Evelyn's high-pitched scream.

The pistol slipped from Lady Sudley's hand and hit the floor with a clunk. She plastered her hands to her mouth and dropped to her knees. "Oh, Lord. What have I done?" she cried.

Elliot raced to the door. Leo groaned as he lay stretched out, a trickle of blood running down his cheek.

"Bloody hell!" Elliot yelled as he joined Alexander and Evelyn at Leo's side.

"Oh, no," Grace called out from the doorway. "Will … will he be all right?"

Mrs. Jones rushed past them. "I'll go and fetch some clean water."

Alexander handed Evelyn a handkerchief, and she patted the obvious mark on the side of Leo's head. "Thank God," she gasped, glancing up at the ceiling and exhaling deeply. "His skin's badly grazed, but there's no wound."

Elliot looked up at the hole in the crumbling plaster. "I think the wall took the brunt of it," he said as relief turned to anger. He jumped to his feet and stormed over to Lady Sudley, who was still sitting huddled in a ball on the floor. "You shot the Marquess of Hartford," he said coldly. "You know what that means."

"I didn't mean to fire. I did not mean to hurt anyone." Lady Sudley looked up at him as she sniffed away her tears. "I can't think. My mind is a blur. Will he live? Tell me he will."

"Oh, he'll live. Thankfully, it is just a superficial wound. But you must answer for what you have done."

Grace came to his side and placed her hand on his sleeve. "You mean to alert a constable? Is there no other alternative?"

After all Lady Sudley had done, Grace wanted him to show clemency.

It beggared belief.

If Caroline were his sister, he would not rest until he'd taken his revenge.

He turned to face her. "What if she'd given your sister an overdose of laudanum? What if she'd lost her child as a consequence? What if the shot had hit Leo in the head? Lady Sudley could have caused the death of three people. I cannot just let her walk out of here as though nothing has happened."

"I know that. But she is just a foolish woman, driven to the brink of insanity by her own perceived inabilities."

Elliot sighed as he pushed his hand through his hair. "There are women thrust from their homes by abusive landlords, left to beg on the streets. Walk through the alleys at night and you'll see men, women, young couples all huddled round a brazier in a bid to keep warm for it's too cold to sleep. Are they not driven to the brink of insanity? Yet do they go around determined to manipulate others for their own ends?"

Grace shook her head. "I know."

The look of sorrow in her eyes was like a spear to his heart. "What do you want me to do, Grace? You can make the choice for your sister. But I must give Leo the opportunity to do what he feels is right."

While Mrs. Jones tended to the abrasion on Leo's head, they spent the time deciding how best to proceed. Alexander and Evelyn were to take Caroline back to Duke Street. Elliot and Grace would escort Lady Sudley back to Hanover Square to wait for her husband. Joined by Mrs. Jones and Leo, they would explain the circumstances to Lord Sudley. They would agree to take no further action if the lady redeemed herself by helping the poor and needy.

"Thank you for doing this." Grace stared into his eyes, and he knew he would do anything in his power to please her. "You have a good heart, Elliot."

It had nothing do with being good or kind. He just couldn't say no to her.

Elliot shrugged. "Based on her reaction, I imagine Lady Sudley would rather spend twenty years in Newgate than face the wrath of her husband."

Grace sighed. "I know what it's like to feel fear at the hands of one's husband. But I know she must pay for what she has done. I'm just thankful we've found Caroline. Do you know if there'll be any lasting effects from the tincture?"

"Once the laudanum has worked its way out of her system, she'll be fine. Caroline's lucky to have you. There are few siblings who would make the sacrifices you have."

She gave a weak smile. "It's strange, but I do not see it as a sacrifice. I have always been there for her and in the process of scouring the ballrooms of London I've met you. Perhaps I should thank her."

Elliot swallowed in a bid to dislodge the boulder-sized lump in his throat. "What will you do now?"

She took a deep breath and her bottom lip quivered. "I … I will need to speak to Caroline. I assume she'll have to come home to Cobham." She stared at a point beyond his shoulder. "Although I'm not sure it will feel like home to me, not anymore."

I love you.

Her words drifted through his mind again, to tempt and to torture him.

"It depends on one's definition of home," he said, his tone melancholic. "Is it the place of one's birth or one's abode? Or is it the place where one's heart belongs?"

He searched her face, her bright blue eyes reminding him of a forget-me-not: wild, vibrant, the emblem of constancy and friendship. He committed the colour to memory, knowing he would never forget her, knowing she was the only woman ever to touch his soul.

A smile touched the corners of her luscious mouth. "Perhaps home has ceased to be a place for me."

He inhaled deeply, calming waves rippling through his body. "Grace, with you—"

"Perhaps I should thank Lady Sudley," Leo said, striding into the room to spoil the beauty of the moment. "You know how the ladies love a scar. I think it makes me look more dastardly, more sinfully dangerous."

Elliot forced a chuckle though his mind was distracted by thoughts of Grace. It would always be Grace. "I'm glad to see you've recovered and feel more like your old self."

It suddenly occurred to him that Leo had not noticed the change in *him*.

He supposed it was not evident outwardly. Yet inside he knew he was not the same man who paraded the ballrooms with his brother, looking for licentious ways to keep memories of the devil woman at bay.

He would never be that man again. But who was he now?

It was a question he could not answer, no matter how hard he tried.

CHAPTER 19

Grace brushed the hair from her sister's brow and straightened the coverlet. "How are you feeling?"

Caroline shuffled up to a sitting position. "Still a little weak, but then I have been in bed for days. It is good of your friends to let me stay here. I couldn't face going back to Arlington Street."

Hours had passed since escorting Lady Sudley home and dawn was fast approaching. Caroline had woken an hour ago and seemed more like her usual self.

"I assume Mr. Henshaw pays the rent on the property?" Grace said.

Caroline nodded. "He did, but Lady Sudley informed me he gave notice before leaving for Europe. The blighter didn't even have the decency to tell me. I should have known he could not be trusted."

Could any man really be trusted?

The events of the last few days had altered her opinion—she could trust Elliot Markham with her life.

Grace perched on the edge of the bed. "Do you remember what happened on the night you went to Hanover Street?" They had only heard snippets from Mrs. Jones and Lady Sudley. "What prompted you to go there?"

Caroline stared at the pink floral wallpaper. "I received a note. I assumed it was from Mark. It had been signed and sealed. But as I had not received a letter before, I had nothing to compare it to. I'd never met him at his home and thought he wanted to talk about the child."

"Was it Lady Sudley who sent you the note asking you to come to Hanover Street?"

Caroline nodded. Grace offered her a drink of tea, but she waved the cup away.

"How was I to know Mark had planned to go abroad?" Caroline pressed the pads of her fingers to her temple and groaned. "Do you know what she said to me? I could hardly believe my ears."

"Lady Sudley wanted you to give her the child you're carrying," Grace said, unable to hide the note of sympathy. "So she could raise it as her own."

"Can you believe it? The woman gave such a pitiful display. I couldn't help but sneer at her desperation."

Caroline was not known for her compassion. Yet, under the circumstances, Grace could understand her sister's frustration.

"Sometimes, in trying to please others, people can make the wrong choices." Indeed, Grace had made a similar mistake. "But in the long term, they only end up hurting themselves."

Caroline's eyes widened, but then she winced and touched her fingers to her temple again. "Don't defend her actions, Grace. The woman is downright evil. Indeed, I was in such a rush to get out of there, I tripped over the rug and banged my head on the corner of the side table. I could have died."

"But thankfully you didn't. It's all done with now. Lord Sudley was furious with his wife and packed her off to the country almost immediately."

Grace swallowed deeply and gave a weak smile as she recalled the look of sheer terror on Lady Sudley's face. It was a look she'd seen in the mirror many times, and it had been painful to watch. Elliot had sensed her sorrow and put his hand to the small of her back. His touch caused all negative feelings to subside, and she'd wanted nothing more than to go home with him and lie in his arms until morning.

"Good," Caroline said, breaking her reverie. "I hope she rots for what she has done to me. I still can't believe you let her get away with it."

Oh, the pain of disappointment, of regret, of feeling unworthy, was far more damning than any physical means of punishment.

"What are your plans now?" Grace asked, ignoring her sister's irate glare.

"Mark is not interested in the child, though I do so want to keep it, Grace." She gave a weary sigh. "I do love him, you know, despite his callous ways. I would never have chosen this life had it not been forced upon me. But I am tired, poor and have no one to offer support here."

For a moment, Grace contemplated offering to stay in London. She could find work as a governess or a paid companion. As a widow, she would not suffer the same fate she feared had befallen Caroline. And she would be free to see Elliot. If he so wished.

"I've decided to return to Cobham," Caroline continued. "I need my family around me." She reached out and took Grace's hand. "I need you with me, Grace. You're so organised and fastidious in your efforts to care for me. If it hadn't been for you, I would still be locked in the attic dosed up on laudanum."

Grace forced a smile, but inside her stomach churned.

"But what of your condition? People may be unkind," Grace said, feeling an urgent need to persuade her sister to change her mind. "How will you cope with it?"

Caroline tutted. "I've been parading about as a courtesan these last six months or more. People have been more than unkind. Besides, I'll have you to fight my battles. My champion warrior. The only person upon whom I can depend."

Guilt and responsibility weighed heavily in Grace's heart. "I shall be sad to leave."

Caroline sat up, a look of fear flashing in her eyes. "You've made some good friends by all accounts. But it is not the same as family. You're to be an aunt, and you've always been so good with children. Don't abandon me, Grace. Not in my greatest hour of need."

What could she say to that?

"When do you wish to return?"

"As soon as possible. I have a few items to collect from Arlington Street. I'm taking all the jewels and clothes, whether Henshaw likes it or not."

Grace nodded. "We could return to Arlington Street tomorrow. Mrs. Whitman will call in on her way back to Cobham. She still believes you're a paid companion. We'll tell her your mistress has gone abroad and won't need your services for a month."

Even though the words were pouring out of her mouth, her mind was engaged with thoughts of Elliot Markham. She would grieve for the loss; she would grieve until she took her last breath.

"Unless you wish to leave sooner." Grace wanted to punch herself on the arm for making the suggestion.

"Sooner?"

"We could ask Elliot—I mean we could ask Lord Markham for the use of his carriage."

Caroline narrowed her gaze. "Whatever he's said to you, it is all lies. It is all a game to win you over. Markham is a man ruled by his voracious appetites. He is crude and vulgar and excels in the art of manipulation. You cannot trust him, Grace." She sighed. "Thank goodness you found me when you did. Perhaps now it's my turn to save you. No. We will return to Arlington Street in the morning and travel with Mrs. Whitman."

Grace had a burning desire to come to Elliot's defence. Caroline was wrong about him. But she knew her sister well enough to know she would never be convinced.

"Very well," Grace said. "I shall go and inform Lady Hale of our intentions. You rest now. You'll need your strength for the journey. Is there anything you need in the meantime?"

Caroline pondered the question. "Perhaps a bath, some perfume, lip rouge and a hot meal. Oh, and a sweet pastry or the like."

Grace forced another smile, although inside her heart was breaking. "I'll see what I can do," she said before heading downstairs to talk to Evelyn.

Evelyn appeared a little shocked at the sudden decision to depart. "We are happy to delay our return to Stony Cross if you would rather stay in London awhile longer. I am sure Elliot would welcome the opportunity to spend more time with you."

"That's extremely kind of you, but trust me, after a full day spent in Caroline's company you'll be shooing us out the door."

Evelyn gave a sad pout. "Does Elliot know of your plans?"

"No." Grace felt a pang of sadness in her chest at the thought of telling him. "I should call around. I told him I would let him know how Caroline fares."

What would she say?

Would he make her an alternative offer or simply accept her decision? Either way, saying goodbye would be like wrenching her heart out.

"Look," Evelyn said. "I have no plans for the day. I may try to catch a few hours' sleep but nothing more. You go and spend some time with Elliot. I shall take care of Caroline in your absence."

Grace shook her head. Evelyn had already done more for her than anyone else her whole life. "I can't ask you to do that."

"You didn't ask. I offered. Now be gone. Elliot won't care if you turn up unannounced."

"If you're sure. I'll wait until after breakfast. It will be safer, and the walk will do me good."

"Katie will accompany you. You can send her back in a hackney." Evelyn stepped forward and took her hands. "Leo said that when you were in the room with Lord Barrington, you told Elliot you loved him. Leo said it worked to calm him, that he believes you spoke the truth."

Grace gripped Evelyn's hands as she could feel the tears welling. "It's true. I did tell him. But it is an impossible situation. Caroline needs me more than ever. I must see her settled before I can think of anything else." Grace sniffed. "Besides, he made no reply. I have no idea what he thinks or feels."

"He loves you. It is obvious to those who know him. But he is set in his ways. No doubt he is struggling with the strange emotion. Go to him. Tell him again," Evelyn urged.

Grace nodded, but she knew she could not commit to him. Not while she had Caroline's problems to deal with. If Elliot truly cared for her, he would wait.

One way or another, and with a heavy heart, she would be forced to leave him.

CHAPTER 20

As the sun rose higher in the morning sky, Grace knew she would find Elliot sheltered in his bedchamber. Whithers left her waiting in the hall while he announced her arrival and she was shown upstairs to the only place she'd ever felt truly happy.

It took a moment for her eyes to become accustomed to the dim light.

"I wasn't sure when you'd come." Elliot crossed the room to greet her, taking her hands in his. His casual dress—a loose white shirt and beige breeches—reflected the way she felt in his company. Comfortable and at ease.

"I'm not disturbing you?" she asked as he stepped behind her to help her out of her pelisse. The pads of his fingers brushed against the exposed skin at her nape, and as she shivered with pleasure, she felt the soft touch of his lips against her skin.

Grace closed her eyes and inhaled deeply. The smell of sandalwood surrounded her, penetrating her clothing, seeping deep into her soul.

If only they could bar the door and never leave. She would be content to spend her days conversing, her nights wrapped in his strong arms.

"My door is always open to you," he said, turning her around and pulling on the silk ribbons of her bonnet. He lifted it gently off her head, all the time his vibrant green eyes staring into hers. She gave him her gloves, and he took all the items and placed them on the wooden chest. "Would you care for something to eat or drink?"

His voice drifted over her like silk: smooth and soft and sensual. The simple question caused desire to ignite—a roaring furnace of emotion flooding her body. Just being in his presence made her head spin, made focusing on anything other than what it felt like to touch him, impossible.

"No," she said, noticing the sinful way his mouth curled at the corners. "I've had breakfast. I don't need anything else."

Only you.

The power of her desire for him shocked her. Even the tips of her fingers were trembling in anticipation. Perhaps it had something to do with the emotional strain she'd endured this last day. Perhaps, with the mystery of Caroline's disappearance now behind her, her emotions were free from guilt.

Or was it because she knew this was goodbye?

A sob caught in the back of her throat and she swallowed to disguise it.

"Your sister is well?" he asked, while his hungry gaze swept over. He wanted her, too. She could feel it radiating from him, the air between them buzzing with a magical force.

"There is much to tell," she said, stepping closer. "But it can wait for now."

A fever burned through her, making her delirious, making her body flame.

She came to stand just a few inches apart, pulled his shirt over his head while he watched with a look of amusement. When her itchy palms settled on his bare chest, the same throbbing sensation that had accompanied her release pulsed in her core.

A pleasurable hum escaped from his lips. "What do you intend to do now?"

Her only coherent thought was that she needed to feel him. She needed to feel full with him. Only him.

She swallowed down her nerves.

This would be the last time.

"I need you, Elliot." She caressed his chest, the dusting of dark hair tickling her palms. "I cannot wait. There's no time." Her breath came in short pants as she fiddled with the buttons on his breeches. Her fingers felt numb. She didn't have the strength to push the buttons through the holes. Frustration surfaced. "I can't do it."

Elliot looked at her and smiled. "Shush." He stroked her cheek, ran his thumb over her bottom lip. "Let me do it."

Feeling a desperate need to hurry, she got to work on the buttons on her dress. Before she began untying her stays, he was already gloriously naked. Magnificently aroused.

"Quick, untie me." She flapped her hands frantically, for no other reason than to speed up the process.

"Love. What's the rush?" he said, freeing her until the only thing standing between them was a thin chemise. "We have all the time in the world."

There was no time.

Time had run out for them.

Throwing her chemise to the floor, she threw herself into his arms. The feel of his body touching hers caused the throbbing to return.

"Don't wait, Elliot."

She claimed his mouth as though she was gasping for air. He made no objection and soon settled in with the wild, erratic pace. Their moans and groans were loud, littered with mumbled curses. Their hands were everywhere, the need to touch sparking an excited frenzy.

Elliot pulled away with a gasp, swept her into his arms and carried her to the bed.

When his body covered hers, she felt no fear, only rapturous joy.

Strangely, she wanted to feel squashed by the weight of him. She wanted his body to surround her, to push her down into the mattress until she could hardly breathe.

He took her mouth instantly, their tongues soon lost in deep exploration. Instinctively, she wrapped her legs around him, squeezing his firm buttocks when she felt the length of his arousal against her inner thigh. He must have interpreted the sign as a need to heighten her pleasure as he trailed kisses along the column of her neck, moving lower still, edging down.

"No," she gasped using the muscles in her legs to hold him in position. This time, she needed to join with him, to feel the soul-deep connection she knew existed between them. "I need you inside me," she added shamelessly, almost choking on the words. There was no time left for modesty.

Elliot practically roared in response and nudged her legs wider. "You make me insane with need."

He entered her in one long, deep, delicious thrust.

Their mutual hum of appreciation rang out through the room. The muscles in her core drew him in, hugged him tight, never wanting to let him go.

Remember this, she said to herself, knowing she would revisit the moment many times in her dreams. *Remember the smell and taste of his skin. Remember what it feels like to be so in love nothing else matters.*

With him buried so deep, the pace shifted.

The urgency subsided, as though they were both where they needed to be, where they belonged. She felt him withdraw only to fill her again, sliding slowly, the sensual movement sending waves of ecstasy coursing through her veins. Rolling his hips to rub against her, he stared deep into her eyes, letting her see the pleasure on his face, giving her everything of himself.

Her love for him burst through her like a bright beacon. But she could not let the words fall from her lips. Instead, she wrapped her legs more firmly around him, poured every ounce of feeling into mirroring his motions to heighten the sensation.

Every slow thrust drew her closer to the heavenly place. But she wanted to hover on the brink, to prolong the moment.

"Oh, God, Grace. I … I can't wait."

Elliot's words sent her hurling over the edge. Pure and explosive, her release shattered through her, the muscles in her core clamping round him, holding him now and forever. She shuddered as the tremors continued to pulse. Then his breath came in a long, satisfied groan and he stilled as he joined her in blissful paradise.

There had been few moments in Elliot's life where words failed to describe his emotion. If fact, that was a lie. He could think of no other time, except for now. Various words sprang to mind: *elation*, *exaltation*, *lust*, *longing*—all of them inadequate. All of them fell hopelessly short of describing the joy he felt swelling in his chest.

He glanced down at Grace. Her brilliant blue eyes were hazy with sated desire, her heavy lids revealing an inner calm. Her warm limbs were wrapped around him, enveloping him, holding him.

Hell, he could live like this forever.

But he sensed that would not be the case.

This was goodbye.

Attuned to her thoughts and feelings, he knew she intended to return to Cobham. She'd not spoken the words, but they were there in the desperate way she'd kissed him. They were evident in the way she held him so tight to her body as though they would be fused as one and as such there could be no separation.

He moved to roll off her, but she kept him anchored there.

"Not yet" came the softest, sweetest words he'd ever heard.

That was another lie. *I love you* had claimed that coveted prize.

Delicate fingers traced a line down his back. "Just wait a little longer."

How could he refuse?

"I'm not squashing you?" he asked, just to distract his mind from a host of chaotic thoughts.

"No." She gave a low chuckle. "I like it. I like feeling close to you."

They stayed like that until a certain part of his anatomy decided otherwise. When he rolled onto his side to pull her into his arms, he realised she was asleep.

The slow rise and fall of her chest against his, the enchanting sound as she exhaled softly, would stay with him always.

It occurred to him to ask her to stay. In what capacity, he did not know. He was not likely to propose marriage. And he gave a quiet snort to show the ridiculousness of that idea. But she deserved better than to be regarded as some gentleman's lover.

There seemed to be no answer to the problem.

Had he been thinking selfishly, with his cock as opposed to his heart, he would persuade her to stay. But he could not become another Henry Denton. He would not make promises he could not keep.

What if all he felt was a more complex version of lust?

When it wore off, how would he feel about her then?

While she ignored his monstrous affliction, would the endless restrictions grate on her?

Would she grow to resent him?

Question after question bombarded his mind until it hurt to think. Gazing longingly at the woman in his arms, he kissed her tenderly on the forehead and the mouth. The selfish act being the only way to soothe him.

As soon as his lips touched hers, she kissed him back in the same gentle manner.

"I did not mean to wake you" came yet another lie.

"I did not mean to fall asleep." She yawned and arched her back as she stretched, her full breasts pushing against him. "I've not slept since I left you last night."

A deep sense of anguish drifted over him, and he knew he should broach the subject of Caroline and Cobham. "Has your sister said what she intends to do?"

She cuddled into him. "She wants to keep the child. She wants to return to Cobham."

He kissed the top of her head, closed his eyes and inhaled the smell of her hair. A smell unique and perfect, a scent that could not be defined. "And what will you do?"

"Caroline will need help when the child arrives. I fear she'll not cope on her own. She has never been one to embrace the practical aspects of life."

"And so you've decided to offer yourself as the sacrificial lamb once again." He knew his words held a trace of contempt and disapproval, but anger and frustration would have it no other way.

She looked up at him, tears welling. "She needs me. After all she's been through, how can I refuse? Besides, I have nowhere else to go."

Guilt slashed at his heart. "Stay here," he blurted, and from the flicker of hope in her eyes, he knew she had mistaken his intention. "Stay in London," he corrected. "Evelyn's aunt won't be back from India for months. I'm sure she won't mind if you stay there. And it will give us a chance to see how this attraction between us develops."

He wasn't surprised to find the glimmer of hope replaced with disappointment. To his own ears, it made their relationship sound superficial. As though it amounted to nothing more than a casual opportunity to ease a physical need.

"I'd like you to stay," he added. It was the best he could do.

She smiled, albeit weakly. "Perhaps placing some distance between us will help you to determine how you feel. You seem confused. I understand that. But I have responsibilities."

"Pandering to your sister's whims will only make matters worse." He knew his sour mood stemmed from the pain searing his heart.

"I don't want to spend the little time I have left with you arguing about Caroline."

A low chuckle escaped from his lips. "You make it sound as though you're leaving tomorrow. But you're right. I don't want to fight with you, Grace."

She placed her palm over his heart, covering the devil's mark. "Elliot, I am leaving tomorrow."

It was as though all the air had been sucked from his body causing a huge cavernous hole to open up in his gut. He pulled her tighter to his chest and wrapped his arms around her.

"Damn it all, Grace. Must you leave so soon?"

Pulling away from him to cup his cheek, she wiggled up and brushed her lips across his, letting the tip of her tongue trace the seam. "Show me that you care, Elliot. Spend our last few hours together showing me that this meant something to you."

While he struggled to say the words she needed to hear, he had no issue conveying his emotion when it came to the pleasures of the flesh.

"I'll happily show you what you mean to me," he said, feeling a burst of desire mingled with a feeling of despair.

CHAPTER 21

There were some things a man would never forget: the smell and softness of a woman's skin, the moment he realised a chaste kiss had the power to heal his soul. The moment he let love slip through his fingers leaving him with nothing but the bitter taste of regret.

"You're not still brooding for Mrs. Denton?" Leo slapped him on the back as they wandered through Viscount Thorpe's crowded ballroom.

"Do not call her Mrs. Denton." Elliot could hear the venom in his own voice. He knew his countenance reflected his pain and misery. "Her husband was a liar and a scoundrel. She deserves better than to carry that blackguard's name."

He sounded overly dramatic. But he refused to see Grace as any man's property.

Not even his own.

The two weeks without her had been torture. Wherever he went, whatever he did, he would catch her unique scent floating past as though carried on a summer breeze. Feeling a sudden rush of excitement, he would swing around expecting to see her face light up the room. But he was always disappointed; he was always alone.

Alexander had gone, too.

At least *he* understood his torment. Alexander knew what it was to love a woman with all one's heart and soul.

Damnation.

Why hadn't he realised sooner?

Why had it taken the pain of separation to come to terms with his feelings?

"Look." Elliot stopped and turned to face his friend. "I think I'll go home. There's no point me being here as my sour mood will only ruin your evening."

Leo's eyes widened. "Don't go. You promised you'd come. You promised you'd make every effort to enjoy yourself." His friend sounded like a possessive wife. "You haven't even been here for five minutes."

Elliot pulled out his pocket watch, checked the time and replaced it. "It's been twenty minutes. Trust me. That's long enough."

"What the hell's wrong with you?" Leo threw his hands up and shook his head. "So, you have feelings for Mrs. … for Grace. The way I see it, you have two choices. Run after the woman and beg for forgiveness, plead for her hand or whatever it is you want. Or find someone here tonight happy to partake in a little amorous sport. There's nothing like a pair of cushioned thighs to make one forget their woes. You taught me that."

"Then you've been taught by a man who has the logic of a donkey," he sneered.

Leo chuckled. "Perhaps the word *ass* is far more appropriate."

"Whether I'm a donkey or an ass, both options are out of the question."

The first option posed a problem beyond his control. Grace insisted on staying with her sister in blasted Cobham. He suddenly decided he detested the place, even though he'd only passed through there once. Grace was loyal and kind. She would not forsake someone in their hour of need.

Besides, what would he do there?

After spending a few minutes in Caroline Rosemond's company, he'd probably end up throttling the woman. Even if his patience prevailed, he'd not be able to hold his tongue. He would chastise Grace for pandering to her precious sister's fanciful notions. They would argue. He'd leave. That would be the end of the matter.

Bitterness and resentment were stoking the fire of his overactive imagination.

The second option was incomprehensible.

The thought of laying his hands on any other woman made him want to scrub his skin raw until it bled. The thought of tangling tongues with anyone other than Grace made him nauseous.

Did this mean he was destined to spend all eternity taking himself in hand?

"I think Melinda Jefferies has taken a shine to you." Leo's light-hearted banter broke his reverie. "She's giving you a look that says 'lift up my skirt and take me now.' Mr. Jefferies has gone abroad, and I hear she is frightfully lonely."

"Are you not tired of it all?" Elliot waved his hand about the room to show his disdain. "When all is said and done, we are alone, Leo. Do you think Melinda Jefferies will give a damn about me once I've satisfied her craving? Do you think any of them would give me a second thought if I were destitute, had a limp or a bulbous nose?"

Leo pursed his lips, but a chuckle escaped. "Forgive me. I did not mean to laugh. It's just my mind conjured an image of you having a nose so large it smothered your entire face."

"Can you not be serious for a moment?"

Leo inclined his head. "We've always known they don't give a damn. We've never given a damn, either. You have always shied away from commitment. No complications. No false promises. Isn't that what you said?"

"Then I have been a fool. One stupid enough to wear bells

and entertain the king's court. I never expected to find someone who would accept our affliction. I have spent my life behaving selfishly—"

"That's simply not true," Leo contested. "You have always been there for me. Like a true brother. And without your assistance, Alexander would not be married to Evelyn. I'm certain of it."

"But don't you see," Elliot said, gripping his friend's shoulder. "It is those benevolent acts that make me worthy of love. Every licentious act eradicates every decent thing I've ever done."

"If that's the case, I am doomed to live as a scoundrel."

Elliot gave a weak smile. "I have changed, Leo. And I cannot go back."

Leo sighed. "Then you have no choice but to go forward."

"You make it sound so easy. I feel as though I am teetering on a precipice. Whichever way I look, I see nothing but darkness. Nothing but doubt and uncertainty."

"One thing is certain," Leo said in a melancholic tone. "Things will never be the same. Not as they used to be. You have been my constant companion these last few years. But what will I do here without you?"

Elliot smiled. He could not sacrifice his own happiness just to keep his friend company. "Find love, Leo. Find someone who makes your heart feel light and free. Someone who loves you despite the beast that dwells inside. Only then can we claim victory over the Bavarian devil."

"That golden-haired snake has done this," Leo suddenly blurted with a level of vehemence that surprised him. "You're afraid. You're afraid of being alone because of your affliction. I swear if she were here I would not stop until I'd made her pay for what she's done to us."

Elliot cast a sympathetic smile. "The only thing I'm afraid of is losing Grace. I'm in love with her. I will wait a lifetime for her if need be. I'm not interested in anyone or anything else. But we will always be brothers. My home is your home. Nothing can break the connection or the bond that exists between us. Yes, we have paid dearly for those nights in Bavaria. But we have gained something precious in the process. Friendship and love and loyalty. Qualities I may never have possessed had it not been for our terrible affliction."

In the crowded ballroom, Leo threw his arms around him. "Then you must go to Cobham, my friend." He pulled away and grasped Elliot's upper arms. "You must fight for your love as you fought to save me, as you fought for Alexander and Evelyn."

Elliot felt a wave of sadness wash over him. "What will you do?"

"I shall do as you suggest. I do have something in mind," Leo replied cryptically. "I, too, must have a purpose. And when I have achieved my objective, I shall come visit you, wherever that may be. Now, get yourself off home and leave me to drown my sorrows between Melinda Jefferies' padded thighs."

Elliot grinned, but then the corners of his mouth drooped. "You will be all right? Tell me you'll not satisfy your thirst on the Season's most coveted debutante?"

Leo waved him away. "I'm over that. I have my sights set on a much greater prize. But I'll tell you more when I see you next."

A sudden sense of foreboding flared, but Elliot pushed it aside believing it stemmed from his reluctance to say goodbye. "We will see each other soon," he said to reassure himself more than Leo. "Wish me luck."

"You don't need it. Grace loves you. I heard the words from her own lips. I could feel it radiate from her like a beacon."

"I pray you're right."

After embracing Leo once more, Elliot left Viscount Thorpe's ball with a renewed sense of optimism. Before leaving for Stony Cross, Evelyn had told him of Grace's love for the countryside. She had intimated he could spend his time between

London and Yorkshire. Hell, the staff at Moorscroft would have a fit of apoplexy if he informed them he intended to take up residency. Some adjustments would need to be made. With any luck, Grace would help him deal with the traumas associated with his affliction.

As he climbed into his carriage, two questions pushed to the fore.

Would Grace consent to be his wife?

Would she choose love over loyalty?

CHAPTER 22

"No matter what I eat it all tastes awfully strange," Caroline said, turning her nose up at her dinner. She pushed the plate away with a look of disgust. "Unless it's fish. Yet that makes my stomach grumble so loud it sounds like there's a bear trapped inside."

Grace glanced at their mother, pleased that she had sat with them this evening. Since returning home after tending to her infirm aunt, she had been distant, far too quiet. Caroline's news had come as a huge shock and a bitter disappointment, not that her sister cared. Caroline had no shame and mentioned her condition at every opportunity.

Indeed, her sister's constant complaining was beginning to grate.

"It's as though Cook has sprinkled a thousand iron filings over the beef and all I can taste is gritty metal," Caroline continued. She glanced across at Grace. "You're quiet this evening. Are you going to tell us what's wrong?"

Grace feigned surprise as she had no intention of discussing her dilemma with anyone. "Wrong? Nothing is wrong. I am perfectly fine. The beef tastes like beef and so what have I to complain about?"

Caroline narrowed her gaze until her eyes were but beady round holes. "You've not been yourself of late. If something is troubling you, you only need say." Her hand flew to her chest. She stuck out her tongue and grimaced as though she'd been foolish enough to suck on a slice of lemon. "Oh, it's revolting."

"Caroline," their mother said by way of a reprimand. "Must you behave so crudely when we're seated at the table?"

Caroline inclined her head. "Forgive me. I'm sure I shall get used to it."

Grace brought her napkin to her lips, which was an excuse to smell the sandalwood shaving soap she'd rubbed into the skin on the inside of her wrists.

As she inhaled deeply, an image of Elliot flooded her mind. Her heart swelled with love, her soul cried out in anguish.

She could cope in the daytime.

Caroline kept her busy, demanding to bathe every morning and evening, wanting her hair brushed a hundred times, convinced it was the only way to prevent it losing its lustre.

Grace didn't have the strength to argue. Her body moved in a series of mechanical motions yet some fundamental part of her was missing. A part of her still dwelled in London, in a bedchamber in Portman Square.

The nights were an entirely different matter.

The nights were unbearable. Sleep eluded her. Even when she managed to drift off, Elliot bombarded her dreams with his handsome face and witty remarks. The pain upon waking—only to realise it had all been a figment of her wild imagination—was often worse than the pain of living with the knowledge she had lost her one true love.

Grace put her hand to her chest, covering the place where Elliot's letter lay trapped between her heart and her stays. If only things were different, she thought, as she glanced at the mantel clock. They had sat down to eat at seven, but Caroline complained it was still far too early and had delayed the meal even further by eating slowly in a bid to keep the food down.

Grace's mind drifted back to the moment she had opened Elliot's letter. The bold, elegant script was so characteristic of the gentleman who had stolen her heart. He had opened his heart to her, offered marriage, declared his love. Just thinking of the words made her chest swell with unbelievable joy.

But what he had given with one hand, he had taken away with the other.

To marry Elliot, she would be marrying a man with a terrible affliction. To spend her life with the man she loved, she would have to leave Cobham, leave Caroline. Elliot could not risk his condition being discovered. He needed routine, a safe place to settle. A place where the sustenance he needed to stave off the cravings was readily available.

Elliot's instructions were clear.

To accept him, she must meet his carriage tonight at nine o'clock, outside the church in Cobham. They were to elope, reside in Yorkshire for the time being.

With every deafening tick of the clock, panic, fear, misery and a profound sadness took root. The chimes for eight thirty were akin to a death knell. The sound indicated the end of all her hopes and dreams.

"I feel so tired I can barely keep my eyes open," Caroline said, bringing Grace back to the present. "And look at the time," she added just to torture her all the more. "In London, the night is just beginning, yet it feels too quiet in the country to contemplate anything other than sleep."

Grace glanced at the clock. With the lanes being so muddy, it would take at least twenty minutes to reach the church. She shook her head dismissively. She hadn't even packed a thing. Besides, what sort of person would she be to put her own needs before that of her sister?

No. She must think of the unborn child—a poor, innocent babe. Caroline would never manage to raise the child without her help.

"Why not get yourself off to bed?" their mother said. She looked tired and weary, too. "You've got a busy day tomorrow, and you'll need your strength. More so, seeing you've hardly eaten a morsel this evening."

"Why? What's happening tomorrow?" Grace asked. In her world, tomorrow was the first day of a life without love. A day where Elliot would know she did not have the courage or strength to choose him.

"Oh, I haven't had a chance to tell you," Caroline said with some enthusiasm. "Mr. Kerridge is calling. I'm to go with him to take a tour of the manor. Mother's coming, too. I didn't mention it before as I thought you had too much to do here."

Grace frowned. "Mr. Kerridge? The squire from Whiteley?"

"Indeed." Caroline clapped her hands together.

"Why would you want to see the manor? You've been there numerous times over the years."

Caroline's eyes grew wide. "I'm taking a tour with a view to accepting a proposal. Mr. Kerridge has asked me to be his wife. Can you believe it?"

All the life was instantly sucked from Grace's body. Her dry lips stuck to her gums. A solid lump pulsed in her throat, and she swallowed in an attempt to clear it. "I … I know Mr. Kerridge has always admired you, but he is thirty years your senior. And … and what of the child you carry?"

Mother groaned. "Must we discuss matters of such a personal nature over dinner?" she said, though her words lacked conviction.

"But I would live in the manor, Grace." Caroline's smile suddenly faded. "But you must not speak of the child. Mr. Kerridge knows, of course. He is desperate for a son, and I have promised to bear his children if he agrees to raise this one as his own."

Grace struggled to absorb the information. Why the hell hadn't she mentioned it sooner? Even an hour sooner would have sufficed. "What of me, Caroline? Have you considered that?"

"Oh, I shall still need you, Grace. You can help me pick new drapes for my bedchamber. And you must come and stay and keep me company when Mr. Kerridge is away."

Anger flared, and she could feel her cheeks flame. "Pick new drapes? Pick new drapes! You mean my whole life has been left in tatters so I can spend my days perusing yards of material?"

"Calm yourself. You're just hurt because I didn't tell you before. Surely you must see the logic in my decision? Surely you don't want me to spend the rest of my life stuck here in Cobham all alone?"

Rage gave way to an uncontrollable feeling of panic and her gaze shot to the mantel clock.

She had less than ten minutes to reach the church. She'd never make it. But she would damn well try.

Grace stood, throwing her napkin onto the table as she inclined her head. "If you will excuse me," she said before striding towards the dining room door. "I have somewhere else I need to be."

There was no time to pack.

After grabbing her cape and retying the laces on her boots, she ran out of the house.

Navigating the muddy lane was almost an impossible task, but determination prevailed. Lifting her skirt, she ran as fast as her feet would allow, trying her best not to slip and dirty the only dress she would have to her name. She ran until her breath burned in her chest. She ran until she had no choice but to stop, clutch her stomach and gasp for air.

Please wait, Elliot.

Despite the fact time was against her, she refused to accept all was lost. But as she came upon the church, relief turned to gut-wrenching anguish.

The lane was empty.

She was too late.

It took all her effort not to sag to the floor in a heap and sob.

In despair, she glanced to the heavens and cried, "Please, Elliot. Please don't leave without me." She hugged her stomach to ease the pain, closed her eyes and repeated the sorrowful words. "I know I don't deserve you. I know I've been such a fool. But I love you. I know you can hear me."

"I can hear you, Grace. There's no need to shout."

Her frantic gaze searched the darkness, falling to the figure leaning against a tree just inside the churchyard.

"Elliot?"

He straightened and sauntered towards her wearing an arrogant grin. "I'm pleased to see my presence still leaves you breathless."

He'd waited.

Her heart swelled so full she thought she might burst. The weeks of separation had been unbearable, and she ran into his open arms.

The kiss was long, slow, a melding of mouths, of hearts and souls.

"You waited," she whispered as she broke away.

"I couldn't leave without you." He brushed the hair from her face. "Had you not come by sunrise I fear I would have been burned to a cinder."

"Don't say that." She hugged him just to prove she wasn't dreaming. "Where's your carriage?"

"A little further along the lane. It's far too muddy along here, and Gibbs was worried about getting stuck in the ditch. I felt a few drops of rain and decided to shelter under the tree."

Tears welled in her eyes, a mixture of joy and fear for the thought of how close she'd come to losing him. "I love you," she said softly. "I want to be with you always. I don't care about anything else."

He ran his thumbs beneath her lids, wiping away her tears as he cupped her face. "Don't cry. You should be happy to know that you're loved. I am so in love with you it hurts. Can you forgive me for being such a stubborn fool?"

"I would forgive you anything."

He took her hand, threaded it through his arm and led her down the lane. "Come," he said, opening the door to his carriage and helping her inside. "I need to get you out of Cobham before you change your mind."

"I'll never change my mind. I'm afraid you're stuck with me now."

He climbed inside. "That's a prospect I'm looking forward to tremendously," he said with a sinful grin as he closed the door and the carriage lurched forward.

"Where are we going?" she asked, settling back into the seat.

"Scotland."

"Scotland?"

"I know it will take more than a week, but it's still the quickest and safest way of making you my wife."

Grace chuckled. "Couldn't you have just petitioned for a special licence?"

"What and risk your sister turning up and dragging you back to Cobham? No. Scotland it is."

Grace removed her cape and placed it on the seat next to her. "You do know that I left in such a hurry this is the only dress I possess."

"Then we should do our utmost to ensure it doesn't get creased." His gaze drifted languidly over her, and she could feel his desire warm her like the heat from a flame. "Luckily, we'll have to spend an awful lot of time alone in this carriage. A shortage of clothing should not cause too much of a problem."

An image of his naked body, all hard and glorious, flashed into her mind, and her desire for him spiralled.

Grace moistened her lips. "What on earth will we do to pass the time?"

Elliot tapped his chest and then glanced left and right. "I thought I'd brought some playing cards."

"I've always loved playing games," she said, sliding across the carriage and falling into his lap. "It requires a certain skill, a level of endurance."

"From what I recall, you are rather talented when it comes to amusing activities."

Grace smiled. "I'm sure there's still a lot more you can teach me."

EPILOGUE

MOORSCROFT HALL, YORKSHIRE

Grace mumbled an endearment as she pressed her naked body against his. He loved watching her sleep. The feel of her warm breath breezing against his skin soothed his soul.

Elliot had kept the fire burning in the grate as they lay on the rug in the master bedchamber. Even though he knew it must be noon, in their private domain, the closed shutters and the thick drapes they'd moved from the drawing room gave the impression it was closer to midnight.

He angled his book of sonnets in an attempt to catch the light from the flames. But he was adept at reading in the darkness. As he turned the page, Grace shifted again, pushing her tempting body closer as her palm came to rest over his heart.

Damn.

Desire sparked.

He could not get enough of his wife—of her charming countenance, of her witty conversation, of her luscious body.

Desire shot through him again when the pads of her fingers traced a circle in the dusting of hair on his chest.

The minx.

"I know you're not asleep," he said, but then regretted his words as he had missed a perfect opportunity to tease her.

Grace gave a pleasurable sigh as she rubbed against him in her feigned slumber.

Elliot placed his book on the floor behind him and rolled onto his side to give Grace Markham his undivided attention.

When his fingers trailed a slow, seductive line down her back, her eyelids fluttered. When those same fingers settled on a deliciously round buttock, her eyes flew open.

"So, you are awake," he said with a grin as he let her feel the evidence of his arousal.

"I am now," she whispered, arching her back as she stretched her limbs. She glanced around the room. "How long have I been asleep?"

"A few hours."

"That long? It feels like minutes."

"Are you hungry?"

She writhed against him. "Only for you."

Taking that as an invitation, he rolled on top of her and settled between her soft thighs. When it came to his wife, he was permanently aroused. "You once told me that home ceased being a place for you," he said as she pulled him closer, urging him to enter her welcoming body.

"I did," she replied, her breath a little ragged. She wrapped her legs around him and rocked to mimic the motion of his first expected thrust.

After spending three glorious weeks together, he could read the language of her body now. Sometimes, she needed him to show his love in slow, tender strokes. Other times, such as now, it would be quick, yet wild, deep, a frantic coupling that would leave them gasping for breath.

"You are home for me, Grace," he said as he entered her fully, unable to suppress the groan of blissful appreciation. "This is the only place I belong."

She panted as she drew him in, as he thrust long and hard and deep. "And you are home for me."

The loud rap on the door ruined his rhythm. While he tried to ignore it, he felt his wife's enthusiasm wane.

"Are you going to see who it is?"

"No," he barked. "They can damn well wait. Just imagine it's the banging of the bedpost."

Her eyes widened—and not with pleasure. "I can't continue knowing someone's listening at the door."

He heard an odd scraping noise and Grace strained to look over his shoulder. "There's a letter on the floor," she whispered. "A servant must have pushed it under the door."

Elliot squeezed his eyes together as he focused on maintaining his erection. "Can't we just forget about it? Go back to where we were a moment ago?"

"But it must be important." A look of panic flashed across her face. "What if it's from Caroline wanting to bring Mr. Kerridge to stay? We can't let them come here."

Bloody hell.

All the blood drained from his face, and from a vital part of his anatomy, too. With some reluctance, but with little option, he withdrew from his wife's warm body and sauntered over to the door.

The first thing that struck him was someone had indeed scrawled the word *urgent* on the front of the missive. Elliot broke the seal, his eyes darting to the bottom of the paper, fearing the worst.

"Thank the Lord," he said, putting his hand on his chest. "It's from Alexander. I had visions of your sister arriving within the hour."

Grace sat up, her soft, full breasts and rosy pink nipples capturing his attention.

"Well," she said with some frustration. "What does it say?"

Elliot scanned the letter as he walked towards her. He almost crumpled to the floor in shock, and he shook his head and read it again.

"What is it?" she asked as he came to sit on the floor at her side. "Your face is deathly pale. Has … has someone died?"

Elliot swallowed. "God, I hope not." Shock gave way to anger. He flapped the letter wildly in the air. "What the bloody hell is he thinking?"

"Who? What? Elliot, will you tell me what is going on?"

"It's Leo," he said, still struggling to believe what he'd read. "He … he's gone, Grace. He's gone to Bavaria."

Saying the words out loud made it sound even more ludicrous.

"Bavaria? Why on earth would he want to go back there?" She shook her head. "There must be some mistake."

Damn it all.

"I sensed something was not right with him. But I was so intent on winning your hand I pushed it aside."

She placed her hand on his arm. "You cannot blame yourself, Elliot."

He closed his eyes and took a deep breath as he recalled Leo's comment about needing to find a purpose and his vehemence for the golden-haired devil.

"He wrote to Alexander. It was delivered a week after his departure." The lump in his throat pounded. "He has gone to Bavaria to seek revenge on the woman responsible for our affliction."

Grace looked horrified. "You think he means to punish her in some way?"

"No. I think he means to kill her. That's why he wrote to Alexander and not to me. He knew what I would do. The bond between us is too strong for me just to sit back and let it happen."

She scrambled into his arms, and he hugged her tight to his chest.

Elliot cursed Leo for his stupidity. But he knew what he had to do.

Grace knew it, too. He could feel her trembling; he could feel the fear in her heart.

"You're going after him, aren't you?" Her voice sounded strained. "You're going to go to Bavaria and try to find him?" She looked up at him, her face ashen, her eyes awash with unshed tears. "Tell me I'm wrong. Tell me you won't go."

Elliot touched his forehead to hers. "I have no choice, Grace. Hell, I don't want to leave you. But I cannot abandon Leo to that monster."

He felt a sudden wave of determination flow through her, watched her straighten as if her spine were a rod of iron. "Then I am coming with you."

"The hell you are. I need to know you're safe else I shall go out of my mind with worry."

She stroked his chest in a seductive rhythm. "Elliot, I have waited my whole life to find you. I am not saying goodbye to you now. Not after all we've been through."

He was a lucky man indeed to have met someone so courageous, so loving, so selfless. But he could not risk losing her.

"No, Grace. It is out of the question. Besides, Alexander is to accompany me."

Her mouth dropped open but then snapped shut as a confident smile formed. "Evelyn will not let Alexander go without her. If Evelyn is going, then so am I."

Elliot shook his head to reinforce his position. "You're not thinking clearly. We are talking about a three-week journey, made all the more difficult by the nature of my affliction. My carriage is equipped for such a purpose, but it will be far from comfortable."

Grace cupped his cheek and forced him to look at her. "I would sleep on a bed of nettles if it meant being with you. I just want to be with you."

He lowered his head and brushed his lips across hers.

"You may come with me as far as London," he said. His desire for her made him weak. "Evelyn can stay with you in Portman Square while you await our return."

She came up on her knees and threw her leg across his lap to straddle him. "And what if Evelyn is to accompany Alexander?" She rubbed against him as she claimed his mouth in the wanton way she usually did when testing his resolve.

He had never been a man to fall prey to the cunning wiles of women. But he had never been a man madly in love.

"All right," he said, breaking contact as desire raged through his veins. He imagined being thrown in the stocks while every honourable gentleman in England threw rotten vegetables at him for putting up such a poor fight. "But only on the proviso, Evelyn accompanies Alexander."

"Agreed." She gave a curt nod and a satisfied grin. "We should pack lightly. Thankfully, I'm used to travelling with minimal clothing."

"We can't leave until dark. I shall be pacing the floor by then."

"Then let us find a way to ease our woes while we wait," she said, moving to nuzzle his neck. Even his despair over Leo couldn't keep his passion for her at bay. Indeed, he was more than ready to spend an hour or two in ignorant bliss.

Three weeks spent worrying about Leo would drive him to the brink of insanity. Perhaps having Grace with him would ease the burden. She could not come as far as Schiltach.

He could not risk her meeting the golden-haired devil.

Thank you for reading ***Slave to the Night***.

If you enjoyed this book, please consider leaving a review at the online bookseller of your choice.

~

Discover more about the author at
www.adeleclee.com

~

If you would like to read an excerpt from the next book in The Brotherhood Series

Abandoned to the Night

please turn the page.

ABANDONED TO THE NIGHT

A gentleman with a hunger for revenge …

A lady with nothing left to lose …

CHAPTER 1

A TAVERN IN SCHILTACH, BAVARIA, 1820

Leo Devlin stared out of his bedchamber window at the dimly lit street below. The first faint ripples appeared in the puddles, spots of rain that would soon make the muddy thoroughfare impassable.

Peering out over the canopy of fir trees lining the hills before him, he could see the outline of the castle's conical spire thrusting up towards the heavens. He sneered at the irony of it all. Did the Lord know Satan carried out evil atrocities just a short distance from his door?

With the thick black clouds heralding a heavy downpour, the streets were deserted, abandoned. All the wooden shutters on the windows had been closed in anticipation of the storm. His was the only face pressed to the glass, the only one desperate enough not to fear the weather.

The stillness of the night surrounded him, penetrated his clothes to seep into his bones. But his heart had been empty for weeks. Even the fair-haired woman warming his bed had failed to bring the relief he desired.

And he knew who to blame.

Leo glanced over his shoulder at the sleeping maid. It wasn't the first time he had joined with her. But she had been the last woman he'd taken as a mortal man and consequently he had a burning desire to compare the two experiences. Most amorous encounters were barely memorable, but the memory of the night he'd been turned was seared into his brain—up until the moment the devil woman had spoken her mystical words and sent him tumbling into a deep sleep.

The screech of an owl drew his attention back to scanning the desolate road.

Two nights he had waited for her to come to the tavern. He had laid his trap. Like the night she'd sunk her sharp fangs into his neck, he frolicked with buxom wenches, was openly crude, walked the lonely streets with his usual arrogant swagger.

Nothing.

No sign of his quarry.

He contemplated strolling up to the castle and rapping on the door, act the wandering stranger seeking sanctuary after being caught in the unexpected storm. Would her servants notice the sword strapped to his back? Would they question him, be quick enough to stop him exacting his revenge?

With some reluctance, Leo pushed away from the window. A warrior was only as good as the weapon he wielded. He walked over to the crude wooden bed, stretched his arm out under its base, tapping the dusty boards until his hand settled on the cold metal handle. A frisson of excitement coursed through him as he pulled it out from its hiding place.

The weary maid did not stir.

The slicing sound penetrated the silence as he drew the sword from its scabbard. He held it up to parry with an invisible opponent, twisting his hand to examine the way the blade cut through the air with ease. The candle flame flickered on the reflective surface. The beauty of the polished steel forced him to catch his breath. Leo had fought many men. He'd sliced through linen, scratched skin, but had never cut deep into flesh. Calvino tutored in the art of swordsmanship as a sport, not with the intention of using it as a lethal weapon.

It seemed a shame to sully the metal, to spoil it with her tainted blood.

But he would make the devil woman pay for what she had done. He would do whatever it took to prevent her from building an army of night-walking monsters.

The distant rumbling outside forced him to move back to the window. The thunder sounded more like a growling snarl as the first crack of lightning flashed behind the castle's spire.

Had the Bavarian temptress felt his presence? Did she know of his plan; could she feel the depth of his disdain?

Leo tried to listen for threads of her thoughts, but with his mind plagued by feelings of bitterness and resentment he could barely hear his own internal voice.

A flicker in the corner of his eye caught his attention. This time, the rumbling came from the wheels of a carriage. His heart lurched at the familiar sight. He would know the blood-red conveyance and the black team of four, anywhere. It haunted him during his waking hours. If he were able to sleep, he knew it would appear in his nightmares too.

The woman lying sprawled across his bed yawned. "What time is it?"

"Shush." He strode over to her, stroked her cheek, altered his tone as he repeated, "Go back to sleep. Sleep now." He could not risk the maid seeing the sword. She would be quick to regale the tale of the murderous warrior, and he did not want anyone to know of his private business.

"But I'm not tired."

"Shush. You will sleep now. You will sleep until I wake you."

By the time he returned to the window, the carriage had gone. He punched the air in frustration, only stopping when he noticed the grey shadow of a figure hurrying along the street below. Shrouded in a cloak, the person gripped their hood as they battled against the wind.

The pounding in his chest vibrated in his ears, a gasp

catching in his throat as a strand of golden hair whipped around the dark material.

She had come for him.

She had read his thoughts; she knew what he had come to do. The need to maintain her dominance and control was important enough to force her to flee her evil domain and brave the harsh elements.

Leo swallowed down the hard lump as she approached the tavern. His hands were shaking; his racing heart caused him to feel dizzy, a little dazed and disorientated. Perhaps he had underestimated his opponent. Perhaps he would be the one to lose his life tonight.

The Marquess of Hartford defeated by a woman?

Never!

Taking deep breaths to calm his agitated spirit, he focused on the importance of his mission. He would avenge his friends, no matter what the cost.

Shrugging into his coat, followed by the leather back harness, he tightened the straps on his shoulders and sheathed his sword before hiding the evidence beneath a full-length cloak.

When she didn't find him sipping his ale would she be bold enough to come up to his room? Then again—

All thoughts suddenly abandoned him. The golden-haired demon walked past the door and continued along the road.

Was it a trap? Was it her intention to lure him away, out into the night? Would she draw him to the graveyard or to another deserted place where she could bare her teeth and control him with her mind?

Either way, he refused to hide in the shadows.

Leo listened for the sensual voice that had once dragged him from the warmth and security of the tavern, the voice that had promised a wealth of pleasure yet delivered nothing but pain. All he could hear was the maid's soft breathing, the muffled din of the rowdy crowd below.

"I'm coming for you," he whispered.

Making his way downstairs, Leo turned his back on the raucous laughter, boisterous antics, and drunken singing. Sneaking out through the back door, he raised the hood of his cloak as he navigated the dark alley. He almost tripped on the stuffed sack until the mound kicked out and delivered a slurred curse.

Slipping out onto the street, he narrowed his gaze, blinking away the droplets of rain clinging to his lashes. He could see her walking ahead. Her strides were quick and purposeful. It took every ounce of restraint he possessed not to charge up to her and take her head clean off her shoulders.

He should have been ashamed to think of harming a woman, let alone in such a callous, vicious way. But the golden temptress was a devil in disguise—not human. She had no heart, no feelings.

When she stopped and rapped on the door of a house, Leo plastered his back against the wall for fear of her spotting him. He waited until she had gone inside before rushing to peer through the tiny gap in the shutters.

Leo didn't know what he expected to find. Perhaps she had woven her mind magic and held some other unsuspecting peer prisoner, her slave to command. Perhaps she was the thirteenth member of a coven and now sat amongst twelve other witches deciding who would be their next victim.

As he gazed through the diamond-shaped hole in the shutter, he almost stumbled back in shock.

Two things disturbed him deeply.

The devil woman had removed her cape. With her hair no longer hidden, the golden tresses hung in glorious waves down her back. She sat in the chair by the fire as a group of children gathered round. One jumped up onto her lap and hugged her tightly.

"And how did you get that bruise?" she said to a boy who pushed to the front to show her his knee.

Leo strained to hear the conversation.

"Frederick pushed me over."

She turned to another boy. "Is this true, Frederick?"

The boy looked at the floor and nodded.

"Then you must be a gentleman. You must hold your head up and say sorry," she replied firmly.

At her command, the boy straightened and delivered his apology with genuine sentiment.

"And what of you, Edwin?" she said. "What must you say to Frederick?"

Edwin gave a gracious bow. "I accept your apology."

"Excellent," she beamed as another child walked towards her carrying a tray of sweet biscuits.

They all watched as his quarry bit into one and swallowed the tiny piece, a host of wide eyes eagerly awaiting her reaction. Whatever she said, it received a joyous cheer from the excited faces.

In a state of utter bewilderment Leo stepped back.

While he struggled to make sense of it all, he considered the second, most shocking thing. The sight of the golden-haired temptress had caused desire to explode through him like a firework at Vauxhall. The feelings were more powerful, more potent than anything he had ever felt before.

Bloody hell.

As he stepped forward to peer through the window, her gaze drifted to the closed shutters.

She knew he was standing there.

Obviously, she had set a trap, found a way to weaken his position. Devious minds use devious methods, he thought, as he chastised himself for being so fickle. The woman had no heart. Avenging his friends was the only thing that mattered. With a renewed sense of purpose, Leo drew his sword, pressed his back against the wall and waited to confront the golden-haired devil.

Books by Adele Clee

To Save a Sinner

A Curse of the Heart

What Every Lord Wants

The Secret To Your Surrender

A Simple Case of Seduction

Anything for Love Series

What You Desire

What You Propose

What You Deserve

What You Promised

The Brotherhood Series

Lost to the Night

Slave to the Night

Abandoned to the Night

Lured to the Night

Lost Ladies of London

The Mysterious Miss Flint

The Deceptive Lady Darby

The Scandalous Lady Sandford

The Daring Miss Darcy

Avenging Lords

At Last the Rogue Returns

A Wicked Wager

ALSO BY ADELE CLEE

ALSO BY ADELE CLEE

Made in the USA
Middletown, DE
14 July 2019